S0-AAC-780

MILES TAYLOR and the GOLDEN CAPE

ATTACK OF THE ALIEN HORDE

ROBERT VENDITTI   ILLUSTRATED BY DUSTY HIGGINS

SIMON & SCHUSTER BOOKS FOR YOUNG READERS
NEW YORK LONDON TORONTO SYDNEY NEW DELHI

SIMON & SCHUSTER BOOKS FOR YOUNG READERS
An imprint of Simon & Schuster Children's Publishing Division
1230 Avenue of the Americas, New York, New York 10020
This book is a work of fiction. Any references to historical events,
real people, or real places are used fictitiously. Other names, characters, places,
and events are products of the author's imagination, and any resemblance to actual
events or places or persons, living or dead, is entirely coincidental.
Text copyright © 2015 by Robert Venditti
Interior illustrations copyright © 2015 by Dusty Higgins
Cover illustrations copyright © 2016 by Dusty Higgins
All rights reserved, including the right of reproduction in whole or in part in any form.
SIMON & SCHUSTER BOOKS FOR YOUNG READERS
is a trademark of Simon & Schuster, Inc.
For information about special discounts for bulk purchases, please contact Simon &
Schuster Special Sales at 1-866-506-1949 or business@simonandschuster.com.
The Simon & Schuster Speakers Bureau can bring authors to your live event. For
more information or to book an event, contact the Simon & Schuster Speakers
Bureau at 1-866-248-3049 or visit our website at www.simonspeakers.com.
Also available in a Simon & Schuster Books for Young Readers hardcover edition
Interior design by Tom Daly
Cover design by Greg Stadnyk
The text for this book was set in Lomba.
The illustrations for this book were rendered digitally.
Manufactured in the United States of America
0516 MTN
First Simon & Schuster Books for Young Readers paperback edition June 2016
2 4 6 8 10 9 7 5 3 1
The Library of Congress has cataloged the hardcover edition as follows:
Venditti, Robert.
Attack of the alien horde / Robert Venditti ; illustrated by Dusty Higgins.
pages cm — (Miles Taylor and the golden cape)
Summary: After starting at a new school, a nerdy
seventh-grader becomes a reluctant superhero.
ISBN 978-1-4814-0542-3 (hardcover : alk. paper) — ISBN 978-1-4814-0555-3 (pbk)
ISBN 978-1-4814-0556-0 (e-book)
[1. Superheroes—Fiction. 2. Moving, Household—Fiction. 3. Middle schools—
Fiction. 4. Schools—Fiction.] I. Higgins, Dusty, illustrator. II. Title.
III. Title: Attack of the alien horde.
PZ7.V5565At 2015
[Fic]—dc23
2014011354

For my family

—R. V.

For my mom, for reading to me when I couldn't,
and for taking me to the bookstore when I could

—D. H.

PROLOGUE

NO ONE KNOWS WHERE HE CAME FROM OR HOW HE came to be.

Some claim he's the result of a top-secret experiment. Others believe he's a guardian angel. Still others say he's an alien from a distant planet (or at least Roswell, New Mexico).

There's only one thing they know for certain: One October day in 1956, he appeared, a dazzling blur streaking from the sky to stop a holdup at First National Bank in Buckhead. He was like something out of a comic book: fast, strong, invincible, and able to fly. Men were awed. Women swooned. The bad guys fought to no avail. Then he was gone as fast as he'd arrived, the gang of robbers tied to a lamppost the only evidence he'd ever been there at all.

A reporter called him "Gilded" because of the way his gold-colored costume glinted in the sunlight, and the name stuck. From that day forward he has appeared regularly to foil crimes, thwart disasters, and do all the things that comic-book heroes do to save the day.

Except he isn't a comic-book hero. Sure, there are comic books about him. Regular books and TV shows and movies, too—all unauthorized, of course, since he's never agreed to a single interview, and nobody knows how to contact him.

But make no mistake: He's real. He's the Halcyon Hero! The Golden Great! The Twenty-Four-Karat Champion!

In other words, he's the complete, 180-degree opposite of Miles Taylor.

AS MILES TAYLOR WALKED THE HALLS BETWEEN

fifth and sixth periods, it suddenly dawned on him that he was having a good day. A good week, even. It'd be an understatement to say the past two months had been rough, but he was starting to think being the new kid at Chapman Middle School wasn't going to be as bad as he'd feared. Maybe—just maybe—he was going to survive. He approached his locker and slipped his backpack off his shoulders, congratulating himself on his streak of twenty-one consecutive class changes executed without incident, and counting.

That's when he saw the Jammer.

In the world of big-time Georgia youth football, Craig "the Jammer" Logg was known as a prodigy. Legend had it that he registered his first tackle at eleven months of age, when he knocked down a toddler at daycare who mistook Craig's mini Nerf football for a teething ring. Craig had been hitting people ever since. It was his calling. As for Craig's parents, Coach Lineman, and all the Chapman Raiders faithful, their calling was to chant "Logg Jam! Logg Jam!" every time Craig stuffed a running back charging up the middle.

Off the field, Craig's new favorite pastime was making Miles's life miserable, and he excelled at that, too. More important, he knew it, and the Jammer wasn't the sort to let talent go undemonstrated.

Miles stopped dead in his tracks, his mind screaming with alarms like a luxury car dealership caught in a baseball rainstorm. The good news was his locker was only a few feet away, whereas Craig was farther down the hallway. The better news was Craig hadn't noticed Miles yet because he was talking with some of the other kids from the football team. If Miles was quick, he could weave his way through the crowd of loitering students, get to his locker, swap out his books, and head back the way he came without Craig ever knowing he was there.

Miles took a deep breath and made his move.

27-9-39, combination lock opened. *Did he see me?* Miles thought. Backpack unzipped, morning books deposited. *Is he coming over here?* Afternoon books retrieved, backpack zipped closed. *Should I look? Don't look!* Backpack slid onto shoulders, mission completed.

Miles wasn't positive, but he might have set a new record for fastest locker stop. Rushed as he was, he never noticed the paper cup sitting on top of his locker. It was positioned at the edge, so it would tip over the side if the locker door was shut with just the right amount of too hard. Which was exactly what Miles, in his effort to make a clean getaway, did.

splash!

A torrent of warm Coca-Cola fell on Miles's head, followed by the hollow sound of the empty cup hitting the terrazzo floor.

Consecutive class changes executed without incident: Zero.

"*There's* where I left my drink!" someone called out.

A hushed silence fell over the hallway, and Miles sensed dozens of pairs of eyes watching him. Wishing he could crawl inside his locker, he instead slowly turned around to find Craig towering over him.

Craig sported feet the size of bread loaves and a head as hard and large as a football helmet—even when he wasn't wearing one. In between was a body huge enough to make neither look awkward. Whenever another football mom asked Mrs. Logg if Craig had been a big baby, she'd reply, "Honey, I thought I was going to *die.*"

Craig bent over and picked up the cup. "It was full when I put it up there," he said. He looked down into the space where sixteen ounces of soda used to be, but now only a few drops remained. "Looks like you owe me a refill."

One of Craig's teammates chuckled. Miles wasn't

sure which one—it could've been any of them, since the only thing that seemed to differentiate them from one another were their jersey numbers. Several other kids joined in, and soon everyone was laughing in unison, as though a Coke falling on someone's head was the pinnacle of comedy. Soda found its way under Miles's collar and trickled down his back.

Among the gathered students were popular kids, like Craig and his pals, who laughed at Miles because that's what popular kids do when one of their own pulls a prank. There were regular kids, too, who laughed because it was what the popular kids were doing. Lastly, there were unpopular kids, who laughed out of relief because it could just as easily be any one of them about to spend the rest of their day sticking to their clothes.

It was a standard post-prank scene, and Miles took it all in stride. He was used to it. Thanks to the Jammer, he'd been in this position many times before, and he was sure he'd find himself in it again. The only thing that would bother Miles was if he saw . . .

Josie Campobasso.

Hers didn't sound like the name of a person, but like the name of a faraway place Miles would only ever see on a map. She was a legend of her own, the girl with chestnut hair and hazel eyes who Miles had heard tales about even at his old school. His first day at Chapman, he spied her at her locker, and Miles knew who she was even before her friend called Josie by name. Georgia just wasn't big enough to have two girls that beautiful.

Josie looked every bit as beautiful now—even surrounded by the pretty, popular girls she was friends with—and Miles wanted nothing more than for her to not see him standing there with soda soaking into his sneakers. But there she was, hair pushed back in a headband, so he could look directly into her clear, bright eyes. A small hummingbird brooch was pinned to her sweater, as if she were letting Miles know that, like a hummingbird, she was always on the wing. Something to gaze upon, but never touch.

Josie didn't laugh with her friends. She didn't shrug indifferently and walk off, the way girls sometimes do when boys are being boys. No, what she did was much worse: She blushed. Her cheeks bloomed red, as though seeing Miles drenched in Coca-Cola had somehow embarrassed her, or rather made her feel embarrassed on Miles's behalf. She felt sorry for him.

The thought of it brought the red out in Miles's own face. Not because he was embarrassed or sorry. He was furious.

"Well?" Craig sneered. "Pay up." He wiggled the cup, beckoning Miles to drop the cost of a refill inside.

What happened next surprised everyone, most of all Miles. One moment Craig was holding the cup, and the next it was sailing through the air.

The hallway fell silent. An unpopular kid wheezed. Craig stared dumbly at his hand, stunned by the cup's sudden disappearance. Miles could relate. If his palm hadn't been stinging from slapping the back of Craig's hand, he would've sworn the cup had gone airborne all on its own.

"Dude . . . ?" one of Craig's teammates said expectantly. He nodded in Miles's direction, an invitation for Craig to dispense punishment. Not that the Jammer ever needed an invitation.

Craig balled his hands into tight fists. He glared at Miles and growled through gritted teeth. "You little—"

"*Mis*-ter *Tay*-lor!" a voice boomed, with stern emphasis placed on the first syllable in each word.

Assistant Principal Harangue was standing in the middle of the hallway. Mr. Harangue was a squat man not much taller than many of Miles's fellow seventh graders, but what he lacked in height he made up for in bulk. He was thick and barrel-chested, and Miles had never seen him without his shirtsleeves rolled up. He probably kept them that way even during the dead of winter, Miles guessed, because the dark hair matting his Popeye forearms would keep them warm enough. Mr. Harangue was the kind of guy whose five-o'clock shadow arrived every day at ten a.m. sharp.

Miles noticed a splatter of soda on Mr. Harangue's

pressed white shirt and looked down to see the empty cup on the ground at his feet.

"Young man, you will deposit that cup in the trash where it belongs," he bellowed, pointing to a trio of nearby garbage bins. Miles wondered whether the wax-coated cup belonged with the recyclable paper or the general waste, but he didn't think this was the best time to ask. "Then you will report to my office and sign up for detention."

Miles was no stranger to Coach Lineman's after-school detention. If asked, Coach Lineman would describe Miles as a troublemaker in desperate need of the discipline one acquires only through the dedicated pursuit of organized sports. In his defense, Miles would say that life was like one of Coach's games, where the referee never sees the player who pushes first but always seems to get his head around in time to throw the flag at the player who pushes back.

School hadn't always been this way for Miles, but it'd been this way since his first day at Chapman Middle. Miles was dealt the hand of being the new kid when his mom fell in with a rich CPA and ran off to start a new life in Hollywood (Florida, that is). Miles's dad held on to the family home for a few months, but he didn't earn enough as an electrician to cover the bills, so he and Miles had moved during the summer between sixth and seventh grades. Just like that, the house where Miles had lived since birth was replaced by a cramped, two-bedroom apartment located in the next school district over.

The distance from old school to new was only a few miles, but for a kid too young to drive it might as well have been the other side of the state. Gone were the friendships he'd nurtured since his first day of kindergarten. In their place were new faces and a new social ladder to climb, starting at the bottom rung.

The familiar surroundings were gone, too. It had taken him days to memorize the layout of his new school. He'd spent weeks learning the hard way which menu items the lunch staff was particularly bad at cooking. Chapman even smelled different, more ammonia-on-steroids and less the soothing, piny aroma that wafted through the halls of his former school.

Not that he'd ever been the big man on campus. But there was a time when he at least recognized the kids at the bus stop, a time when someone would save him a seat in the cafeteria if he got stuck at the end of the lunch line. At Chapman he was alone.

Miles glanced at the clock above the multimedia screen and slumped back in his chair. Ten more minutes, and he'd be paroled. Looking around, Miles sized up some of the other kids in detention and tried to guess what had brought them there.

Seated in the desk to his right was Jeff Jeffries, with his long stringy hair and wearing a faded black T-shirt. Head of the school's metalhead faction, Jeff had flunked two grades in elementary school, so he was one of the oldest kids at Chapman—old enough for his parents to let him ride the MARTA downtown with his nineteen-year-old brother to see whatever death-metal band was playing, even if it was a school night. Probably got busted for sleeping in class, Miles thought.

To Miles's left was Trisha Brevard, the bubbly captain of the Raiders cheerleading squad. Her shrill voice was a constant, and not just at football games. She always had something to say about nothing in particular, even during class, when the only person who's supposed to be saying anything is the teacher. Detention had seemed to quiet her, though. With no one in the room worth talking to, she instead texted her friends for news from the outside world.

Travis Bramlett was at the back of the room, twirling his pencil like a hunting knife. A scrappy kid with a mean streak, Travis didn't care much for music or sports. He didn't care much for authority, either, an attitude that more often than not landed him in detention. Not that Travis cared. The only thing Travis cared about was making sure the boys didn't try to date his little sister, a pretty sixth grader named Trina. As long as Travis shared a school with her, Miles doubted anyone would go near her.

It surprised Miles how much he knew about the others. He supposed that was what reputations did—outline the necessary details that made each kid different from everyone else, kind of like social cheat sheets. But there was one kid in detention whom Miles had never seen before.

Miles could tell from the textbooks on the kid's desk that he was enrolled in seventh-grade classes, but he looked too young to be in the sixth grade, never mind the seventh. Small wasn't the word. He was tiny, as underweight as he was undersized, like a full-sun shrub that had spent its whole life in the shade. The only large thing about him was his glasses, which must've been too heavy for his face because he kept pushing them back up his nose.

You can't blame a kid for his physical shortcomings—having small parents with bad eyes wasn't his fault—but the way he dressed himself only made things worse. His yellow polo shirt was belted into khaki pants that, amazingly, were too small even for him. Sitting down made them ride ridiculously high on his ankles, exposing crisp, white tube socks and a pair of off-brand sneakers so white and shiny that they must've just come out of the box. He dressed the way cool kids dressed back in the days of . . . Actually, there was never a time when cool kids dressed that way.

Worst of all—the absolute worst—the kid was reading a comic book. No, not reading. Studying. He was hunched over, face close to the comic and his lips moving silently as he recited the word balloons to himself. Its pages were worn and bent from countless readings, and the whole thing looked as though it were on the verge of falling apart altogether.

And it wasn't a cool comic book, either, something science fiction or crime. It was an issue of *Gilded Age*, the sappy superhero monthly about Gilded's latest heroic deeds. Sure, Gilded was awesome. He was the only for-real superhero the world had ever known. But if you wanted to know what he was up to, all you had to do was catch thirty seconds of news. Just this morning, Miles had eaten toaster waffles while the TV aired the previous night's highlights of Gilded in action. He'd rescued a family caught in a burning house, then blown out the fire with one puff of air. Miles remembered having a tougher time blowing out the twelve candles on his last birthday cake.

The kid was setting off a major nerd-alert. He was so harmless to look at, Miles couldn't imagine him doing anything bad enough to merit detention. Then again, the only thing Miles had been guilty of was not having a single friend to testify on his behalf in front of Mr. Harangue.

Coach Lineman glanced at his stopwatch, the same stopwatch he frowned over in PE whenever someone failed to finish their half-mile run in less than five minutes (something Miles was always guilty of). He folded his sports section, tucked it in his armpit, and stood from his chair.

"Time!" he announced, clicking the stopwatch with his thumb.

Everyone made their way toward the door. Jeff Jeffries strolled past, iPod blaring loud enough for Miles to hear screaming guitars. Trisha Brevard dialed her cell phone. Travis Bramlett yawned.

Miles thought he was the last one to leave the room, but on his way out he looked back and saw the tiny kid with the glasses still hunched over his comic book, absorbed in every detail.

CHAPTER
2

MILES'S BUS HAD LONG SINCE LOADED UP AND GONE
by the time detention let out, so his dad was waiting
in his work truck at the curb.

Hollis Taylor had started working for Atlanta
Voltco as an electrician's apprentice right out of high
school. Over the years he'd advanced to master's status, and one of the perks that came with the title was
a white Ford pickup from the company motor pool.
The truck was battered and scratched, and the uphol-
stery was torn from years of electricians—Mr. Taylor
included—sitting down with screwdrivers still in their
back pockets. But Mr. Taylor had earned the right to
drive it, and he couldn't have been prouder.

Miles tossed his backpack onto the middle seat
and climbed in. Mr. Taylor dropped the truck into
gear and circled through the parking lot. "How was
school?"

"It was school."

"Right." Mr. Taylor rubbed his beard with one hand, a gesture Miles knew meant his dad wasn't sure what to say. Miles's mom had always handled the heart-to-hearts. "You might not mind it so much, if you steered clear of detention. Shorten the school day a little?"

"It wasn't my fault, Dad." It was a lackluster defense, one Miles had grown tired of repeating.

"It never is. All I'm saying is, it'd be helpful if I could stop ducking out of work to come get you."

"I could ride my bike to school. It'd be safer than the bus, anyway."

Mr. Taylor scoffed. "Not with the traffic in this town."

"Traffic doesn't stick chewed Bubble Yum on your seat."

Miles glanced over at his dad, and for a moment they locked eyes. Both sets were the same bright shade of blue, a source of family pride that Mr. Taylor said went back four generations.

"You know, I was the new kid once," he said. "We had to move because your grandpa changed jobs, so I started high school in a different county than my buddies. It wouldn't have been so bad, but your grandma made me wear a tie on my first day." His expression soured, as though he could taste the bad memory.

Miles chuckled. He couldn't remember ever seeing his dad wear a necktie. Even his parents' wedding photos showed them standing on the banks of the Chattahoochee River, both of them dressed in T-shirts, shorts, and sandals. The pastor wore canoeing attire, too, and after the ceremony they all went downriver together. "Did you get made fun of?"

"Shoot, yeah." Mr. Taylor let out a long, slow whistle. "Fashion back then was faded jeans and hunting jackets. It didn't last long, though."

"How'd you get it to stop?"

"I busted Jimmy Grant's nose playing dodgeball." Mr. Taylor tapped his nose with one index finger and grinned. "Bull's-eye."

"I don't have much of a throwing arm, Dad." Miles slouched in his seat, hopelessness settling in. If sports were the only way to get the Jammer off his back, he was doomed.

The truck slowed to a stop at a red light, brakes squeaking. Mr. Taylor turned toward Miles. "I know life isn't the way we want it right now. If you'd told me a year ago that we'd be where we are, I'd have called you crazy. But here we are, right?"

Miles shrugged.

"We'll get things sorted out, son. You'll see."

The light turned green, and the truck shuddered as Mr. Taylor eased it ahead with the traffic. "Did you at least finish your homework? Or did you sit in detention like a bump on a pickle?"

"I got hung up on the math." Truthfully, Miles hadn't tried to do the day's math assignment yet. Fractions drove him nuts.

Mr. Taylor raised an eyebrow suspiciously. "Well, you can take another crack at it while I work. There are some things that still need doing."

Miles watched the city pass by outside his window. It was late October, the start of his mom's favorite season. Every autumn, usually in mid-November, she'd pack a cooler with sandwiches and drinks, and they'd all drive north on I-75 to Chattanooga and back. She'd "ooh" and "aah" at the changing leaves, splashes of yellow and red and orange amid the evergreens lining the highway. Miles and his dad would scan the tree line to catch a glimpse of turkey or deer. He doubted he and his dad would make the drive alone this year.

Last time they'd talked on the phone, Miles's mom had told him that in Hollywood coats were optional during the winter months, and the swimming pools stayed open year-round. Miles hadn't thought to ask if the leaves that far south ever changed color at all.

They pulled into the downtown construction site just after five o'clock. A chain-link fence surrounded the site, and workers toting loaded tool belts and empty lunch buckets were filing through the gate and heading home for the night. Mr. Taylor drove up to the wooden security booth and rolled down his window.

Out of the booth stepped a security guard with a tarnished silver badge pinned to his shirt and a handheld radio clipped on his belt. He bent down and rested an elbow inside the truck's window. "What're you doing back, Hollis? I thought you knocked off already."

"Tough job," Mr. Taylor said. "I decided to bring in an outside expert." He jabbed a thumb at Miles.

The guard looked over at Miles and smiled. "Going to help, huh? From what I hear, Hollis needs all the backup he can get."

"Be nice, Cliff, or the power in your little house there might not be on tomorrow."

Cliff laughed and waved them through.

Ever since he was little, Miles had been coming to work with his dad. Usually it was just a quick stop to install a new wall socket or replace some faulty wiring. Once, when Mr. Taylor was sent to change a ceiling fixture in a downtown high-rise, Miles got to sit in some big-time CEO's chair.

Other times, like today, they went to construction sites, which were much more fun. Miles enjoyed exploring the skeletons of buildings before the drywall was hung, and there were always scraps of board and lengths of pipe for him to mess around with.

This particular site was a nearly completed concrete parking garage. Not as interesting as some of the other sites he'd been to, but Miles was optimistic he'd find some way to entertain himself until it was time to leave. He jumped down from the truck and bounded off, his eyes scanning the discarded building materials scattered over the ground for anything worthy of closer examination.

"Forgetting something?"

Miles turned to see his dad eyeing him sternly. His tool belt was already buckled around his waist, and in one hand he held his flashlight. With his other hand, he held forward Miles's backpack, waiting for him to come take it.

"I'll do my math when I get home," Miles pleaded. "I swear."

"Not a chance. You burned me with that one last time."

Miles trudged over and followed his dad inside the ground floor of the garage. Mr. Taylor set the backpack down on a makeshift table fashioned from a section of plywood set across a pair of metal sawhorses. The table was coated in sawdust, and nails and empty soda bottles were strewn about.

"You can set up here," Mr. Taylor said. He pulled over a battered, paint-splattered stool that, from the looks of it, had seen more construction sites in its lifetime than Miles had. "If you need me, I'll be in the circuit breaker room at the other end of this level. I won't be long." Mr. Taylor walked off.

Miles plopped onto the stool. The days grew shorter in the early weeks of autumn, and downtown, where the sun hid behind the Atlanta skyscrapers, the days felt shorter still. He could barely make out the circuit breaker room hidden in the long shadows at the far end of the garage.

Miles took out his math book and opened it to the day's assignment. The page was a mishmash of numerators and denominators. He sighed and reached into the backpack's front pocket for a pencil.

boom

Thunder? Miles hadn't seen any rain clouds on his way to the site. Storms often rolled in without warning in Georgia, but that usually happened during the spring and summer months.

Boom

The sound was getting closer. Maybe it was a C-130 cargo plane returning to Dobbins Air Reserve Base northwest of the city. The roar of a C-130's engines could rattle your eardrums, especially downtown, where the concrete echoed the sound.

BOOM

The parking garage shook, sending dust down from the overhead beams. There was no way thunder was making that noise. A plane engine wasn't, either. Miles rose from the stool, curious what the source might be. Besides, who could multiply fractions with all that racket going on?

B-BOOM!

The structure shook more violently, and this time the tremor was followed by a loud, metallic *clang!* It came from inside the garage, from the same area as the circuit breaker room.

"Dad!"

Miles ran to the room, worried his dad had fallen off a ladder. He saw bundles of rebar toppled over, pinning the door to the circuit breaker room closed. "Dad!" he shouted. "You okay?"

Mr. Taylor's muffled voice yelled back from the other side of the door. "I'm fine. What in the *heck* is going on out there?"

"Everything just started shaking. Like there was an earthquake or something."

"This is Georgia, son. There aren't any earthquakes. There's probably a road crew grading the street." Miles heard his dad shoulder the door.

wump

And again.

wump

"Why won't the door open?" Mr. Taylor hollered in aggravation.

"There's some rebar in the way." Miles tried lifting one of the bundles, but it wouldn't budge. "I can't move it," he grunted. "It's too heavy."

Mr. Taylor cursed under his breath. "All right. Don't hurt yourself. Go to the guard shack and get Cliff. Then wait for me in the truck. I don't want anything falling on your head."

Miles walked back to the table and stuffed his math book into his backpack.

B-BOOOM!

The rumble nearly knocked Miles off his feet. He gripped the table to steady himself.

Miles should've done what his dad told him—ask Cliff for help and go to the truck where he'd be safe. But parking garages were safe, too, right? Garages like this one were built to support the weight of hundreds of cars. Thousands, even. What could be safer than that? Besides, if it was only a grader, there was nothing to be worried about. Miles just wanted to see for himself. The noise was so close . . .

B-BOOOM!!!

Miles slipped his backpack over his shoulders and stepped slowly toward the edge of the garage. He didn't spot any road crews on the street. No graders, either. Maybe it was just a thunderstorm after all. He placed his hands on the short concrete wall and leaned out, so he could see the sky.

Miles stared at the old man lying where Gilded was only moments before. The battle against the creature had killed him. But how? Gilded couldn't be killed. In all the years that he'd battled crooks and fires and floods, he'd never even been hurt.

Miles picked up the golden cape. The fabric— or whatever it was made of—vibrated lightly in his hands. Even with the garage cloaked in late-afternoon shadow, the cape glinted as though it was in the noonday sun. It didn't reflect light; it emitted its own.

That's when it dawned on Miles: Gilded wasn't an experiment or an angel. He wasn't even an alien, though today's events were sure to convince people otherwise. He was human, and he always had been. He didn't have powers. The cape did. And that meant—

"Hollis! Kid! You in here?"

Cliff's voice snapped Miles out of his daydream. He was shaking with adrenaline. He threw off his backpack and tried putting the cape inside, but it was as long as a grown-up's raincoat. It wouldn't fit.

Cliff's footsteps were getting closer. Any second he was going to discover Miles holding a supercharged poncho.

Miles didn't have time to think. He flipped the backpack upside down and dumped his books on the ground. He crammed the cape inside and zipped the backpack closed.

"Hello?" Cliff called out again. "Anybody hear me?"

"Over here!" Miles shouted back.

Cliff hustled over. "Dang, kid. You coulda been killed." He surveyed the pile of rubble, and when he saw the old man, his face went pale. When he saw the creature, it went paler. "You didn't touch that thing, did you?"

Miles shook his head emphatically. "No way."

Cliff fumbled at a small holster on his belt. He took out a canister of pepper spray and pointed it at the creature with a shaky hand. "Is it . . . dead?"

"I think so. It hasn't moved." Miles noticed dark green blood pooling around the creature, and his stomach rolled over. Apparently, the sight of monster blood made him queasy. "What is it?"

"It ain't good. I can tell you that. Where's your old man?"

"Trapped in the circuit breaker room. The door is blocked."

Cliff started to return the pepper spray to its holster, glanced at the creature again, and then thought better of it. "Follow me," he said, backing away. "Let's go get him."

Miles was frozen in place. Something about the creature's dying expression filled him with dread. Its mouth hung open in a grotesque, jagged snarl that displayed its sharp, yellow fangs. He couldn't tell if the expression was a grimace, or a grin.

"Come on, kid," Cliff admonished. "Your dad wouldn't like you near that thing."

Fear sent a shiver down Miles's backbone. He didn't want to look at the creature anymore—he wanted to get as far away from it as possible—but he couldn't stop staring. It was dead—Miles was sure of it—but it was as though he was worried it was only playing possum and would come back to life as soon as he turned away.

Miles took one last, lingering look. Then he hurried after Cliff, unable to shake the feeling that he'd come face-to-face with that snarl again.

CHAPTER 3

THE FIRE DEPARTMENT WAS FIRST ON THE SCENE.
It took two men to free Mr. Taylor from the circuit breaker room, but not until after they'd spent a good, long while gawking at the dead creature. People trapped in rooms were a daily occurrence for firefighters. The carcass of a reptile-alien mash-up that had ridden into town on a flying sleigh? Not so much.

Mr. Taylor emerged from the room with a frown. He noticed the firefighters and the flashing lights of the ladder truck parked at the end of the garage. Embarrassed, he rubbed his face with one hand. "Sorry, guys," he groaned. "I didn't mean for my boy to call nine-one-one."

One of the firefighters blinked. "Nobody called us. We're here because of . . . well . . . because of *that*." He turned and pointed back toward the rubble pile. Several firefighters were standing around the creature, debating what they were supposed to do next. One of them poked at it gingerly with a snapped-off length of two-by-four. Miles guessed that was as close to checking its vital signs as they were going to get.

Mr. Taylor's mouth fell open. "What the . . . ?"

"If you're all right, we're probably needed elsewhere." The firefighter waited for Mr. Taylor to answer, then gave up and trotted off to join the others.

Miles followed as his dad walked slowly toward the creature. Outside the garage, police cars and fire engines were blocking off the parts of Peachtree Street that had been damaged in the attack. Paramedics loaded bandaged people into the backs of ambulances. Most of the injuries didn't look too bad—after Gilded had arrived, the creature's rage had shifted to him instead of the afternoon commuters—but it'd be a long time before downtown was fully repaired and back to normal.

Mr. Taylor wheeled on Miles suddenly. "This is why I told you to wait in the truck!" he yelled, as though he'd known all along that an extraterrestrial incursion was imminent and his pickup was the safest place in the universe. He grabbed Miles by the shoulders and spun him around, examining him from head to toe. "Anything broke?"

"I'm fine, Dad." Miles could tell that his dad wasn't mad. He was scared.

"Thank the Lord." Relieved, Mr. Taylor let out a long exhale. "Trouble always seems to track you down, doesn't it?"

Miles wanted to point out that, had he been allowed to do his homework later like he'd asked, he wouldn't have been anywhere near where he was when the roof caved in. But before he had a chance, Cliff brought over an older, round-bellied man with a bald head and wire-rimmed glasses. He wore a dark blue uniform, not a fire suit and boots like the other firefighters.

"This the kid you were telling me about?" the man asked Cliff.

"That's him. Name's Miles Taylor."

The man looked Miles in the eye. "Hello, Miles. I'm Fire Chief Malcolm Willingham. Can you tell me what happened here?"

Miles was taken aback. An adult asking for his side of the story? This was something new. "I was doing my homework," he said. "I heard a loud noise coming from outside. I went over to look, and that's when they crashed through the roof."

"They?" Chief Willingham raised an eyebrow. "You mean Gilded and the, uh . . ." He waggled a hand in the creature's direction, trying to come up with a word for it. "You know."

"Yes, sir."

"What about the other guy? The old man. You see him?"

"No, sir." Miles shifted his feet. "I mean, yeah, I saw him on the pile. But I didn't see where he came from."

Chief Willingham watched a pair of EMTs load the old man's body onto a gurney. It was covered with a sheet, so Miles couldn't see his face. Not that it mattered—he wouldn't be forgetting that face anytime soon.

"He was on top of the rubble," Chief Willingham said sadly, "so he probably came from one of the upper floors. We didn't find any ID on him. Could be he's homeless."

"I've had to chase a few people out of here," Cliff offered. "I don't recognize him, though."

Chief Willingham turned back to Miles. "And what about Gilded? He fly off?"

Miles grabbed the straps of his backpack, adjusting the weight on his shoulders. "Yeah. I mean, *yes*, sir."

Chief Willingham patted Miles on the head. "Oh, I think we can forgive you for being a little informal. Frankly, I don't think any of us know how to act right now. It's been a . . . strange day."

Mr. Taylor placed his hands on Miles's shoulders. "If you don't mind, I'd like to take my son home now."

"Sure thing. But, Miles?" Chief Willingham's

expression softened into an easy smile. "Next time, do your homework at home. It's safer."

Miles was beginning to like this guy.

Miles and Mr. Taylor headed for the work truck. News helicopters from the local networks and even CNN—their headquarters was only a mile away—hovered overhead. They jockeyed for position in the sky, each of them trying to get a perfect shot down through the hole in the parking garage. If they weren't careful, they were going to crash into one another and become part of the six-o'clock news, instead of just covering it.

As they were driving out of the construction site, Mr. Taylor had to swerve to make room for a line of army vehicles heading in the opposite direction. An olive-green Humvee was followed by more than a dozen transport trucks with canvas tops and armed soldiers seated in the back. The lead vehicle stopped, and a tall man in combat fatigues stepped out. He was thin and tanned, and his craggy face was punctuated by a bristly white mustache that hung above his upper lip like a bottle brush.

The man strode over to Chief Willingham and gestured in a way that made it very clear the army was now in charge. To reinforce the point, soldiers carrying rifles began herding Chief Willingham and the other firefighters out of the garage.

Finally, when the last of the trucks had rumbled past, Mr. Taylor steered through the gate and started home.

Deejays were taking calls from frantic listeners insisting that the world was coming to an end. Others phoned in to say it was all a hoax. After cycling through the stations twice in search of someone talking about anything else, Mr. Taylor gave up and clicked off the radio.

"We know it wasn't a hoax, don't we?" he said.

Miles nodded slowly.

"Well, those people saying it's the end of the world don't know any better than the people saying it's a hoax. Because they weren't there. So don't worry about what you hear." He looked at Miles reassuringly. "Besides, we don't have anything to be afraid of, so long as Gilded is around."

Miles wondered how many other parents were telling their kids the same thing at that moment. Mr. Taylor had used the line a million times on Miles, and it had always worked. It weaned him off of his nightlight, ended his fear that there were monsters under his bed, and kept him from having nightmares that time he'd hidden around the corner and listened as his parents watched *Saw*. What kid wouldn't feel safe with a superhero patrolling the skies? An hour ago, the thought would've made Miles feel safe, too. An hour ago.

"What if he wasn't?" Miles gulped. "Around, I mean."

"He is. And it's a good thing, because if he hadn't been there today, then you might've been hurt. Or worse." Mr. Taylor looked away, and his voice grew heavy. "Anyway, he's around. That's all there is to it."

Miles held his backpack tight. He realized for the first time that the city would be depending on him now, and the thought terrified him. He replayed Gilded's words in his head: *You'll figure it out. I did.* Miles didn't know what that meant, but he knew he needed to learn. Fast.

It was well past dark by the time they arrived at Cedar Lake Apartments. The name didn't make much sense, since there was neither a cedar tree nor a lake to be found. The only trees on the property were a pair of crepe myrtles overgrown from years of neglect, and the closest thing to a lake Miles had seen was during a hard rain a few weeks back, when trash had clogged the sewer grates and the parking lot had flooded all the way up to the sidewalks. At least the mallards had enjoyed themselves.

The apartment complex consisted of a pair of two-story stucco buildings facing each other across a cracked asphalt parking area. They were painted beige with dark brown trim, a combination that was intended to blend in, but instead put them in stark contrast with the brightly colored strip malls and fast-food restaurants all around them. Cedar Lake's lone amenity was a Dumpster with a lid that didn't close flush, making it a favorite haunt of the local raccoons. The Taylors were a far cry from the wooded subdivision they'd moved away from.

Miles followed his dad up the concrete stairwell and down to the farthest end of their building. It was the location of apartment 2H that had convinced Mr. Taylor to sign the rental agreement. A second-floor end unit meant they'd have neighbors only on one side and no one above them, so he reasoned it would be as peaceful as an apartment could be. For Miles's part, he was glad his bedroom looked out on the row of Leyland cypresses behind the complex. The same unit in building 1 would've given him a bird's-eye view of the never-ending traffic on Jimmy Carter Boulevard.

Mr. Taylor unlocked the dead bolt and dropped his tool belt onto the wooden chair in the apartment's entranceway. "Hungry? I can fry us up some hot dogs." He pulled a pack of buns from the cupboard, checked the expiration date, and frowned. "Or not." He set the stale buns aside.

Miles couldn't think about eating anyway. His

heart raced as he hurried down the hall. "I'm tired," he called without looking back. He turned into his bedroom and locked the door.

Miles clicked on the bedside lamp. His room was orderly, all his belongings in their proper place. The laundry was in the hamper. His skateboard was under the bed. His globe was on the desk, the continent of Asia facing the room, so he couldn't see Florida on the other side.

Miles knew his tidiness didn't come from his dad, whose life was a never-ending hunt for some misplaced tool or set of keys. All Miles knew was that for as long as he could remember, he'd found comfort in the organization of things. Organization relaxed him. It made him feel in control. The outside world had experienced an attack unlike any it had ever seen, and it would never be the same. Inside Miles's bedroom, however, nothing had changed. Everything was just as it had been when he left for school that morning.

Everything except the contents of his backpack.

Miles carefully set his pack on the nightstand, unzipped the pouch, and peered inside. The cape glowed, just as it had in the parking garage. He took it out and once again felt it vibrating. In the quiet of his room, he realized that when he touched it, he could hear it, too. It emitted a low hum, like a fluorescent lightbulb doing its job. The sound traveled through his body and reverberated in his eardrums. Never did he think he'd be so close to something so magnificent.

Miles was no athlete—just ask Coach Lineman. Still, he was sure that he was faster, stronger, and could jump farther than the old man in the garage. But none of that had prevented the cape from transforming the old man into the greatest hero the world had ever seen. Maybe what they said in those commercials for that local chain of men's stores was true: Clothes really do make the man.

Miles spread the cape flat on the bed. Even though it had been stuffed tight inside his backpack, it hadn't wrinkled. It showed no signs of wear, either—not a single rip or frayed thread despite the battle it had gone through. There wasn't even any grime on it, as though the dirt and concrete dust had simply been unable to stick to it. It was perfect.

Catching a glimpse of his reflection in the full-length mirror nailed to the inside of the closet door, Miles noticed, not for the first time, how utterly average he was. Mouse-brown hair and fair skin. Not too short or too tall, too fat or too thin. He didn't think of himself as ugly, but he certainly wasn't handsome, either. He just was.

Miles carried the cape over to the mirror. The

fabric was thin, but weighty. Solid and substantial. He laid it over his shoulders, holding one half of the clasp in each of his hands so the cape wouldn't slide off. He turned to the side to see how it looked, like he was trying on an outfit in a dressing room. It hung all the way to the floor and bunched up around his feet, but it still looked better than anything he'd ever worn in his life.

Miles rubbed his thumbs across both halves of the clasp, marveling at how smooth and flawless they were. Each half was lined with a part of some kind of curled, alien symbol. He slowly started bringing the pieces together to complete the image. Like magnets, the nearer the two halves came to each other, the more forcefully they pulled themselves even closer. Closer.

"Miles?" Mr. Taylor called from the other side of the bedroom door. "You still awake?"

Startled, Miles dropped the clasp pieces, and the cape fell to the carpet. Mr. Taylor jiggled the locked doorknob. "Come on, son. Open up."

Miles heaved the cape into the closet and shut the door.

The bedroom doorknob jiggled harder and was followed by a loud knock. "Son?" Miles sensed the impatience in his dad's voice.

Miles swung the door open to find his dad

standing in the hall with his arms crossed. "What is it about today?" he fumed. "If I'm not getting stuck in a room, I'm getting stuck out of one."

"Sorry. I guess I locked it on accident."

Mr. Taylor stepped inside and scanned the room suspiciously. His eyes settled on the open backpack. "What're you up to in here?"

"Nothing," Miles answered innocently.

"Mm-hmm." Mr. Taylor motioned at the bed. "Sit. There's something I need to say."

Miles sat and tried to act casual. "If you're worried about me, you don't have to be. I mean, it was kind of a weird day, but I'm okay."

Mr. Taylor sighed and sat beside Miles. "That's because you're a kid. You don't get caught up in thinking about what things mean. But you're twelve now, and the day isn't long off when you'll start seeing the world differently."

Mr. Taylor scratched his beard, searching for the right words. Then he took a deep breath and squared his shoulders. "What I'm trying to say is, life can get pretty darn confusing. I'm here for you, if you ever need to talk. About anything at all."

Considering what was stashed in the closet, Miles had the feeling his version of "anything at all" was a lot different from his dad's. His dad probably thought Miles would want to talk about the creature with the nightmare snarl, or about seeing the old man's body getting wheeled away on a gurney, or even his mom being gone. They still hadn't talked about that one. Not really.

The thing on Miles's mind at the moment, though, he doubted his dad would want to hear: The old Gilded was gone, and for some inexplicable reason he'd picked a seventh grader to fill his golden boots. Miles was tempted to show his dad the cape and see his reaction, but Gilded's warning had been clear. *No one can ever know.* After all the good the hero had done over the years, the least Miles could do was obey.

"I know, Dad. Thanks. I'll, um, let you know if something comes up."

Mr. Taylor's shoulders drooped. Whatever he'd expected Miles to say, clearly it wasn't that. "Okay, then. You know where to find me. Good night."

On his way toward the door, Mr. Taylor stopped and picked up Miles's backpack. He opened the pouch wide and stared down into it. Miles's heart froze. Was there some trace of the cape still inside?

"Guess your books got buried at the site?" Mr. Taylor frowned.

Miles tried not to look as relieved as he felt. "Oh. Yeah."

"In the morning, I'll call the school and tell them

an alien ate your homework. Wouldn't be right, you catching hell for something like that."

"No!" Miles blurted. "I'll handle it. One less hassle for you to deal with, right?" The last thing Miles wanted was people at school quizzing him. Asking what he'd seen at the parking garage. Asking if he'd taken anything with him. Normally he wouldn't have objected to an uptick in his popularity, but that was attention he didn't need.

Mr. Taylor set the backpack down again. "All right, but if they try charging you for the books, I'll have to talk to them. We can't afford that right now."

With one hand on the doorknob, Mr. Taylor turned back to Miles. "Kill that closet light before you turn in." He pointed at the floor, where a patch of gold light beamed from under the closet door. "We can't afford a high power bill, either."

Miles didn't remember his closet having a light.

The bedroom door closed with a click. Miles dashed over to the closet. On the floor next to his sleeping bag and his tackle box, the cape lay in a glowing heap. Apparently, it was capable of doing a lot of things, but camouflaging itself wasn't one of them. He rummaged around for a box or a sack—anything to hide it in—but there wasn't anything. Stashing it in the sleeping bag would have to do for now.

Miles changed into his sleeping shorts, brushed

his teeth, and climbed into bed. He lay in the dark and listened to his dad root around in the fridge, followed by the familiar creak of the sofa springs and the mumble of the living room TV.

Miles was anxious to put on the cape and see what would happen. He'd had it for only an hour, though, and already he'd almost been caught with it. To be safe, he'd wait until after his dad went to bed and try it on then.

But Miles wouldn't get the chance. Exhausted by the day's events, he drifted off to sleep.

LORD COMMANDER CALAMITY SLUMPED DEJECTEDLY on his throne. For years innumerable, he'd been waiting. He was beginning to think he was waiting in vain.

The Lord Commander was the leader of a race who called themselves the Unnd. There was no earthly language that possessed a word capable of describing their culture. The closest any word came was "opposite," meaning "diametrically different or of a contrary kind." Only in the Unnd's case, they weren't the opposite of one thing, but of all things. Or of all good things, at least.

They were the opposite of kindness. They were the opposite of happiness. They were the opposite of generosity and selflessness and basic decency. They were the opposite of all that was right and good— of every positive impulse that any living thing had ever possessed—because those were the trappings of weakness. Selfishness and conceit and downright meanness were the way to true domination, and the Unnd had those traits in spades.

A human might see them and think they were the descendants of some intergalactic species of reptile. They were scaly and sharp-toothed and had small, beady eyes like a snake or a lizard. But their large tusks and concertedly nasty demeanor set them apart as something far more sinister than merely reptilian. Come to think of it, their deadly alien weaponry did, too. In fact, if an Unnd were to stumble upon a snake or a lizard, they would smash it with whatever heavy object was closest at hand and never take note of any similarity between them.

The Unnd were bullies. They were lousy sharers. They were liars with pants ablaze. And their leader was the worst of them all.

Whether the name "Calamity" had been given to the Lord Commander at birth or was one he adopted later in life, none who served under him could say. If it was the former, his parents had a knack for predicting the future, because calamity accompanied the Lord Commander wherever he went, and he instructed the Unnd horde at his command to make it as calamitous as possible.

Especially when it came to the *GGARL!*

Of all the things in the universe that Lord

Commander Calamity and the Unnd were the opposite of, they were the most opposite of their sworn enemies, the *GGARL!* The *GGARL!* were so revoltingly beneficial, so determined to help others, their presence made any Unnd worth its bile want to vomit. And not in a good way.

Since longer than the Unnd could remember, they'd been at war with the *GGARL!* So deep was the Unnd's enmity of the *GGARL!*, their true name had been erased from every Unnd dictionary eons ago, and to speak it aloud was a crime punishable by a most Unnd-pleasant death. They could be referred to only as the *GGARL!*, which wasn't even a word, so much as a sound—a throaty growl that by law must always be accompanied by a clenched fist and followed by spitting on the ground.

The war between the Unnd and the *GGARL!* stretched back so far in time, it predated even the *GGARL!*'s hideous golden capes. For there had been a time when the *GGARL!* didn't possess such technology, and the Unnd were the most powerful force in the universe. No one opposed them, least of all the *GGARL!*, who had nothing but their puny statures and their revolting goodness with which to defend themselves (and, as even the youngest Unnd whelp knew, goodness was no good at all in a fight).

Back then, the Unnd had driven the *GGARL!* from

every planet and star system where they dwelled. The *GGARL!*'s numbers had dwindled, and the Unnd were on the brink of eradicating them from existence altogether. The Lord Commander remembered those days fondly. They were terribly Unnd-happy.

But in their most hopeless hour, the *GGARL!* had proven themselves to be most resourceful. They invented a weapon that was *exceptionally* good in a fight: the golden capes.

The capes granted the *GGARL!* extraordinary abilities. Speed, flight, resilience, and strength that matched any Unnd, even the Lord Commander himself (though he'd never admit it). And those were just the abilities the Lord Commander knew of.

The capes turned the tide in the war. The *GGARL!* began spreading their awful goodness among the planets and star systems again. If many *GGARL!* combined their efforts, no Unnd horde stood a chance against them. Indeed, it was the Unnd who might've been eradicated, if the *GGARL!* hadn't made a single, ill-fated decision.

Believing their numbers were too few to withstand the Unnd forever, the *GGARL!* divided their forces. They dispatched lone scouts in ships to search the universe for allies, other worlds that might use their own technologies to join the side of good and squash the Unnd threat once and for all. In their desperation, Lord Commander Calamity saw opportunity.

The Lord Commander scoured the ranks of his horde for the vilest trackers he could find. Ruthlessness was a prerequisite. Cruelty a positive. Above all, their hatred for the *GGARL!* should be so intense and festering that the very thought of them would throw the trackers into a fit of frothy rage. The trackers must be Unnd-decent in every way.

The Lord Commander cast these trackers among the stars, tasking each of them with a single mission: Track down one of the *GGARL!* scouts and transmit its location to the Lord Commander's waiting horde. Once alerted, the horde would mobilize, and all the Unnd's considerable military might would rush to engage the lone *GGARL!* in unison. Against such a force, not even the protection of a golden cape would be enough. And when the *GGARL!* scout was dead, the Lord Commander would have one of the coveted capes in his grasp.

If a cape could be studied, and Unnd scientists could somehow discover its secrets, then the Lord Commander could make his own arsenal of capes. A horde of Unnd in capes would decimate the *GGARL!* for all time, and the universe would be under the Lord Commander's heel forever. He'd have to pick a different color for his capes, though. The gold used by the *GGARL!* was much too cheerful and decent.

Maybe mauve. The Lord Commander had always been partial to mauve. After all, he wasn't without a sense of fashion.

These were the Unnd-kind thoughts that had consumed Lord Commander Calamity's mind for ages. They consumed his mind even now, as he sat on his horrible throne in the horrible great hall of his horrible fortress. But even amid all of that horribleness, he still wasn't Unnd-satisfied. Because despite all his considerable efforts, not a single *GGARL!* scout had been located. Not one cape was in his possession. And so the universe was not yet his.

"Is e-everything to y-your Unnd-liking, Lord Commander?" A servant bowed low in front of the throne, his entire body quivering with fear.

The Lord Commander tried to recall what planet the servant had come from, but it escaped him. He had conquered so many worlds and subjected so many peoples to servitude that the names and places all ran together. A pity. He wouldn't mind having an entire court of servants like this one, since he was particularly good at quivering. It reminded the Lord Commander of his mother's curdle pudding. Oh, how the Lord Commander pined for his mother's curdle pudding. It was the foulest he'd ever tasted.

"Of course not!" the Lord Commander snarled.

"There are entire star systems still to be conquered. What's there to Unnd-like?"

"A-apologies, Lord G-Gener—"

"Silence! Leave my presence!" The Lord Commander watched the servant slink away, then thought better of it. "But stand where I can still see you quivering."

The doors to the great hall were suddenly thrown open, the sound echoing off the coal-black rock of the walls. Snarlpustule, the chief fortress guard, stood breathless in the opening. "Lord Commander," he hissed. "We've found one."

The Lord Commander sat forward, his jaw tight with humorlessness. "Beware, Snarlpustule. I usually Unnd-encourage cruel pranks, but today I'm in no mood."

Snarlpustule approached the throne. "It's true, Lord Commander. One of the trackers has trans-mitted a signal beacon. They've located a *GGARL!*" Snarlpustule thrust a clenched fist into the air and spat a glob of steaming mucus onto the floor.

"A *GGARL!*" Not to be outdone in his own great hall, the Lord Commander thrust his fist higher and expelled a larger, steamier mucus glob of his own. "What's the tracker's report?"

"No report, Lord Commander. We assume he's been killed dead."

"Who cares!" the Lord Commander bellowed. "If

he fell in battle with a *GGARL!*, it's a most Unnd-deserving death. Where's the cape located?"

Snarlpustule referenced a printout on a scroll of paper. (Technologically advanced as the Unnd were, they still printed everything on paper. They were able to pulp more trees that way.) "Some ball of earth the locals call Earth."

"Earth . . ." the Lord Commander mused. "Not an overly original name. I don't remember that one. Have we conquered it already?"

"I think we flew past it once. The primitive race that inhabits the planet was still living in caves and walking barefoot. You didn't think they'd be very fun to fight."

"No boots?" the Lord Commander inquired. "What do they use to crush things underfoot?" If there were unknown ways to crush things underfoot, he wanted to know about them right away.

"I suspect they don't, Lord Commander."

"No crushing? Hmph. If the *GGARL!* think they can find allies with such a meager race, then they're more desperate than I suspected."

"Indeed, Lord Commander. What are your orders?"

The Lord Commander stood from his throne, his lips pulled back in a ferocious sneer. "Assemble the horde at once. I want the full assault brigade aboard my cruiser. Any warrior who isn't motivated, let them know they're being given the chance to die a warrior's death. We're hunting *GGARL!*" The Lord Commander thrust both hands into the air this time and let loose a mucus glob so large, he was certain it'd be written about for eons to come.

"*GGARL!*" Snarlpustule echoed.

Every warrior in the great hall repeated the cry until the walls shook and the floor was slicker than a professional snot-hockey oval.

Lord Commander Calamity listened to the cacophony, and he was Unnd-moved. At last a cape was within his reach, and nothing was going to stop him.

Especially not the people of Earth. When the Lord Commander was finished with them, they were going to understand the value of boots.

CHAPTER
5

CRASH!

Miles's morning began with the sound of a dish shattering against the wall of the apartment next door.

Mr. and Mrs. Collins lived in unit 2G. Miles had met them both on the day he and his dad moved to Cedar Lake Apartments. It was a sweltering Saturday in July, the type of weather that Mr. Taylor referred to as "angry hot." They hadn't thought to bring a cooler of drinks, and all their cups and glasses were packed away in one of the countless boxes they hadn't thought to label. Not that cups or glasses would've done them much good since the water wasn't turned on.

The U-Haul truck wasn't half-emptied, but Miles and Mr. Taylor were already way more than half-drenched with sweat. The sofa hadn't gone into the apartment without putting up a fight, and Mr. Taylor was on the verge of becoming angry hot himself when there was a light knock on the open front door.

Mrs. Collins introduced herself as their neighbor. She'd brought a serving tray laden with a pitcher of sweet tea and two glasses filled to the brim with glistening ice cubes. Not just any old ice cubes out of an ice machine, either. They were in the shape of little palm trees. She explained that she collected ice cube molds for every holiday and season, and she used the decorative ice only for special occasions.

The tea was delicious. It was home-brewed, but the sugar was completely dissolved, not a syrupy sludge sitting in the bottom of the glass. Mr. Taylor guzzled his first glassful down without once coming up for air. Mrs. Collins took that as a compliment. She reached for the pitcher to pour Mr. Taylor a refill, but Mr. Collins barked for her, and she said she had to go.

For the next ten minutes, Miles and Mr. Taylor sat on the sofa and sipped their tea, pretending they couldn't overhear Mr. Collins scolding his wife. Miles learned three things about Mr. Collins that day: His first name was Tom; he didn't care to have his wife serve sweet tea to another man, whether she was just being neighborly or not; and he liked to yell. A lot.

Miles lay in bed now and listened as Mr. Collins scolded his wife again. It was a common morning occurrence that usually had something to do with Mr. Collins's eggs being too dry, or his cereal being too wet, or some other breakfast-related catastrophe.

Miles felt bad for Mrs. Collins. He liked her, and not just because of her sweet tea and palm-tree ice cubes. She always flashed her kind smile when Miles passed her on his way home from the bus stop, no matter how late she was for her shift waitressing at the Biscuit Barrel.

Miles slid out of bed and pulled on a pair of jeans and a T-shirt. His dad had already gone to work, leaving him to hear Mr. Collins's rant alone.

"What'd you do to the bacon?" he hollered.

"Last time you said it was too fatty," Mrs. Collins answered.

"That don't mean I want it *blowtorched*! Crack a window and let out some of this smoke 'fore it sets off the fire alarm!" There was more crashing of dishes, and Mrs. Collins screamed.

Miles gritted his teeth. He wanted to help, but what could he do? Her husband sounded like a genuine nutjob, the type who kept a Louisville Slugger by the door just in case a neighbor decided to get nosy. At Miles's height, his head would be right in the strike zone.

The cape.

Why didn't he think of it sooner? This was exactly what it was for, right? A Louisville Slugger would be no match for Gilded. And if Gilded came to Mrs. Collins's aid, even a guy as crummy as Mr. Collins would have to admit that it wasn't because she had the superhero on speed dial.

Nervous, Miles walked shakily to the closet. He pulled the cape from the sleeping bag, and its lustrous fabric cascaded to the floor. He draped it over his shoulders, a swarm of butterflies fluttering in his stomach. If the cape granted powers, then it was time to put them to the test.

Miles started bringing the two halves of the clasp together. Just as had happened the night before, he felt them pulling themselves closer.

Miles thought about Mrs. Collins's kind smile. He realized she probably wasn't smiling right now.

Closer.

Was Mr. Collins raising more than his voice?

Closer.

Someone had to help her!

Suddenly, the two halves of the clasp leaped from Miles's hands and fused together with a soft click. The clasp's surface rippled and then went smooth, leaving no trace that it had ever been not whole.

For a heartbeat, Miles felt weightless, like he'd tipped down the hill of a roller coaster, and the track hadn't yet caught up. Then a surge of power rushed into him. He was solid as granite. Strong as gravity. Mighty as the universe itself. He was all those things and more, the power washing over him until—

YOU'D THINK ALL THOSE NIGHTS WORKING AT A *RESTAURANT,* MAYBE YOU'D *GET A CLUE* HOW TO COOK!

NOW LOOK WHAT YOU DONE!

JUST *ONE MORNING* I'D LIKE FOR YOU TO NOT GIVE ME SOMETHING TO *HOLLER* ABOUT!

I'LL TELL YOU THIS:

WHOEVER'S AT THE DOOR, THEY'RE ABOUT TO WISH THEY'D *MINDED THEIR OWN--*

--BUSINESS?

NOW HOLD UP! YOU GOT *NO RIGHT* COMING IN HERE!

SNAP!

HEH.

HEY! PUT ME DOWN!

ARE YOU OKAY, MRS.--

UM, I MEAN, MA'AM?

YEP.

YOU'LL BE NICE TO HER FROM NOW ON, WON'T YOU?

S-SURE.

BECAUSE IF YOU AREN'T, I'LL COME BACK HERE.

AND YOU DO NOT WANT ME COMING BACK HERE, RIGHT?

R-RIGHT.

GOOD. I, UH... GUESS THAT'S IT, THEN.

HAVE A NICE DAY.

BYE.

CLICK

THUD!

Miles lay on his back, relieved he hadn't broken any bones. More good news: He hadn't landed in a blackberry bramble. Some bad news: He *had* landed in a fire ant mound. He rolled across the ground, swatting at the ants and suffering a few bites on his hands in the battle. He stood and brushed the leaves and twigs from his school clothes.

His *school clothes*? How did he end up back in his jeans and T-shirt? Where did the Gilded suit disappear to?

The cape was still around his neck, but something was different. There was no glow, no soft hum. It might as well have been from one of those cheap, off-the-rack imitation Gilded outfits that were so popular on Halloween. He barely touched the clasp, and it split into its two separate halves.

Miles replayed what had happened. One second he was cruising through the air, fantasizing about his plans for seventh-grade domination. The next he was dropping like a stone, the cape's power rushing from him like air from a too-full balloon. Luckily, the protection abilities had been the last thing to go. If not, Miles would've had a lot more to complain about than a few fire ant welts. Or maybe not. It's kind of hard to complain with your guts splattered all over the ground.

Had the cape run out of juice or something? Miles checked for a battery compartment or an electrical socket, but found none. Maybe it needed to recharge itself. After yesterday's workout against the alien, who could blame it for wanting some downtime?

Miles would have to figure that stuff out later. He needed to hustle, or he was going to be late for school and earn himself another afternoon in detention.

CHAPTER

6

TENSION HUNG OVER CHAPMAN MIDDLE LIKE A BLACK cloud. None of the teachers talked about the alien's rampage in downtown, but it was obviously on everyone's mind. In history class, Mrs. Antebellum kept glancing out the window, like she was expecting an attack to level the school at any moment. After having a parking garage nearly come down on top of his head, Miles understood how she felt.

Mrs. Antebellum stayed skittish all throughout her lecture on William Tecumseh Sherman's march to the sea, but Miles didn't pay much attention. Who cared if Sherman had led his Union soldiers right past where Chapman Middle now stood? If the general were still alive, even he'd have to admit that his feats paled in comparison to what Miles could do with the Gilded cape on his shoulders.

Miles had considered leaving the cape at home,

but, come to find out, when he folded it neatly instead of crumpling it into a ball, it fit inside his backpack without any fuss. Score one for the neat and tidy. Folding somehow made the cape weigh less, too, so each time Miles laid the mystery fabric over on itself, it became lighter. Folded all the way down, it wasn't much bigger or heavier than a spiral notebook—still too large to carry in his pocket, but it left plenty of space in his backpack for his textbooks. Or at least it would've, if he hadn't ditched his books at the construction site.

The cape was only a reach away, waiting for Miles to put it on and do . . . What exactly *could* he do with it, anyway? Fly? Check. (Land? Not so check.) The cape definitely made him stronger—he'd snatched up Mr. Collins as if he were stuffed with straw. Miles figured the cape probably let him run fast, too, but how fast? Was he set-a-world-record-in-the-one-hundred-meter-dash fast, or dash-around-the-world-in-under-a-minute fast? Miles tried to think of all the amazing things he'd heard about Gilded doing over the years. If the old Gilded could do it, then it stood to reason Miles could now, too.

Thoughts of the cape swirled in Miles's brain, making it hard for him to concentrate on much of anything. Even scheduled stops at his locker, usually as quick and efficient as a tire change at Talladega, were slowed by a constant feeling that he needed to look over his shoulder to make sure no prying eyes were trying to sneak a peek inside his backpack.

Of course, he could always hide the cape in his locker for safekeeping.

Yeah, right.

Chapman wasn't without its criminal element, and theft was way too common for Miles to entrust the security of the cape to his locker's combination code and flimsy metal hinges. Any thief worth his swag would have a tougher time breaking into a can of Campbell's soup. No. The safest place to keep the cape was with him, in his backpack and on his shoulders at all times.

Which posed a problem when sixth-period PE came around. Miles knew there was no way he'd be allowed to wear his backpack during spud, or muckle, or whatever other tortuous game Coach Lineman planned to inflict on his students for the fifty minutes he was allotted. So Miles did what every other right-thinking adolescent does when they really want to get out of school-mandated exercise: He faked a stomach-ache.

A few winces and a prolonged groan were all it took to convince Coach Lineman to sideline him. Coach enjoyed pushing kids *almost* to the point of puking, but *actual* puking was something he didn't want any part of. Not when the gymnasium floor had recently been rewaxed. He sent Miles to the bleachers with Trisha Brevard, who claimed to be suffering from an "illness" of her own. It didn't seem to slow her texting ability one bit.

"Must be something going around," Miles said with a knowing grin. Trisha rolled her eyes and went right back to texting.

At least the day passed without incident. Miles's teachers never noticed he had come to school without his books. He didn't even have any after-school detention to work off. Maybe the cape also came with good-luck powers.

When the final bell sounded, Miles was the first one out the classroom door. He fast-walked through the halls, bypassing his locker and heading straight for the bus corral. His heart raced with anticipation. How in the world had he managed to sit through an entire school day? But it was over now, and the weekend awaited him. And what an incredible weekend it was going to be.

"How's your tummy, wimp?"

Miles stopped short. He didn't need to look to know who was waiting for him.

The Jammer.

Under normal circumstances, Miles wouldn't have

stopped at all. He would've continued through the exit and out to the buses, pretending he didn't hear Craig's booming taunt. The bus corral, patrolled by drivers and teachers herding kids into their proper transports, was a bully-free zone. Much safer than the chaotic free-for-all indoors.

These weren't normal circumstances, though, and the Jammer was about to find out why.

Miles spun around. Sure enough, there stood Craig with some of his teammates flanking him. Craig held a half-eaten sandwich in one hand. He grinned, his lips parting to reveal peanut-butter-smeared teeth. "You gonna puke, wimp?"

Anger boiled inside Miles like a baking-soda volcano. He clenched his fists and stepped forward, locking eyes with the pride of Chapman Raiders football.

"I look at your face long enough, and I just might."

Craig's grin froze. Miles could almost hear the lummox's meager brain cells working overtime, straining to determine whether or not they should feel insulted.

One of Craig's teammates shook his head sadly, as though he truly felt sorry about what he knew was going to happen next. "Duuude," the kid breathed heavily.

Miles recognized the kid from yesterday's incident

with the soda cup. Apparently, "dude" was the only word in his vocabulary.

Craig's brain cells finally determined that, yes, they should feel insulted. Deciding this was going to be a two-fisted job, Craig stuffed what was left of the peanut butter sandwich into his mouth and swallowed it down in a single gulp.

"I'll give you something to puke about," Craig grunted. He drew back one fist slowly, like he was cocking a catapult.

Miles stood his ground, hands on his hips and chest puffed out. Craig, Dude the Teammate, and everyone else around must've thought he was insane. Nobody voluntarily took a hit from the Jammer, not even if they were wearing full pads and a helmet. Why was the new kid not running away, or at the very least making an effort to protect himself? And why did he have that stupid smile on his face?

None of them knew what Miles knew. *Hey, Jammer,* he thought, as Craig's right fist closed in. *You're about to gut punch a superhero. Good luck not breaking your hand.*

The blow landed with such force, it was as though Craig were trying to swipe the wallet from Miles's back pocket by way of pushing through his body. Miles dropped to his knees, his breath leaving him in a rush. For a moment he was worried he'd never be able to inhale again, but then he rocked back and sucked in a long, squonking breath that sounded like a donkey coming up for air from the bottom of the sea.

Miles recorded a mental note: *Next time, put the cape on before you pick a fight.*

Craig wasn't finished yet. Not wanting his left fist to feel left out, he raised it and took aim at Miles's head. Through squinted eyes, Miles saw what was about to happen. Using every ounce of strength left in him, he lifted his shaking arms and stacked his hands in a T.

"T-t-time out," he stuttered.

It worked. Craig wasn't one to argue with time out. Hitting someone after the referee called time out got you flagged for fifteen yards. He pulled back his punch just before it pounded a divot in Miles's face. Then he stood there, like he was waiting for someone to blow a whistle and let play resume.

Somehow, Miles convinced his legs to stand him up. Clutching his knotted stomach, he looked around and found a bathroom behind him. "Wait here," he said, wincing.

Confused, Craig turned to Dude the Teammate for advice. Dude the Teammate shrugged.

"You got it," Craig said, offering Miles a nod. "Sixty seconds."

Bent over with his stomach still balling, Miles stumbled through the bathroom door. He kneaded the knots from his stomach and straightened himself upright, frowning at himself in the mirror. How could he be so dumb? Toting the cape in his backpack didn't make him Gilded. Wearing it did.

The bathroom was empty. Miles dropped his backpack on the floor and reached inside. He felt the soft hum of the cape's fabric, and the sting of Craig's punch melted away.

Sure, Miles had made a life-threatening error by confronting the Jammer without the cape, but now he was downright giddy, relishing the revenge to come. He started making a mental list of all the different things he was going to do to Craig. Starting off with a punch to the gut was a no-brainer, just to even the score. After that, maybe Miles would drag Craig to the nearest football field and spike him in the end zone a dozen or so times. The possibilities were endless. And the best part? Miles wouldn't even get in trouble for any of it because Gilded would be the one doing it all. What was Mr. Harangue going to do—send a superhero to detention?

Enough relishing. It was time to get down to business. Miles tossed the cape over his shoulders and threw open the bathroom door with a—

WHAM!

Miles stood in the doorway, basking in the amazement of his fellow students. He scanned the crowd, searching for the one person he wanted more than anyone to see him. There, with her friends gaping and gawking around her, he found Josie.

She was stunned. Incredulous. She truly had no idea what she was seeing. The sight of Gilded emerging from the boys' room had understandably made quite an impression. Maybe after he made short work of Craig, Miles would fly her home. No more cramped bus rides for Josie. She was Gilded's girl now.

"Surprised?" Miles announced cockily. "Well, you ain't seen nothing yet!"

Miles leveled a steely gaze at Craig, who was as stunned as everyone else. At least for once there was a reason for him to have a stupid expression.

"Get ready, Jammer! You're about to get . . . jammed!"

Okay, as far as superhero catchphrases went, it needed work, but that wasn't important right now. The important thing was Craig was finally going to get what was coming to him. And then some.

Miles marched toward Craig, his foot stomps echoing in the hushed hallway. He tilted his head back and glared straight up into Craig's . . .

Wait.

Why was Miles still looking *up* at Craig? Shouldn't he be looking *down*? Craig was big, but nowhere near as tall as Gilded. And why wasn't Craig scared? When Mr. Collins had come face-to-face with Gilded, he'd been terrified. Craig wasn't even stunned anymore. If anything, he was smug.

Miles looked down at himself, and to his horror he discovered that he wasn't Gilded at all. No superhero costume. No muscles or strong hands, and probably no steely gaze, either. He was regular old Miles Taylor, with a goofy golden cape thrown in to boot. He reached up for the clasp and felt its two halves hanging loosely. In his hurry to pummel Craig, Miles hadn't noticed that the clasp hadn't connected properly. No wonder everyone was staring. The cape slid off Miles's shoulders and fell silently to the floor.

There was a snicker. Then the crowd erupted. "The new kid thinks he's Gilded!" someone squawked.

"Du-u-u-de," Dude the Teammate guffawed.

Miles wouldn't have blamed Josie if she were laughing, too. Instead she nudged one of her giggling friends with an elbow. "Don't be mean," she said.

Humiliated, Miles scooped up the cape and dashed back into the bathroom. The last thing he heard was Craig's roaring laughter. "Catch you later, super*zero*!"

Alone in the bathroom, Miles threw the cape onto his shoulders again. He tried pushing the clasp together, but it was no use. It wouldn't fuse into one piece the way it had that morning.

Was it possible it hadn't recharged yet? How could that be? Even if the battle against the alien had used up a lot of juice, hadn't Gilded spent an entire day building sandbag dams and helping stranded drivers when a rainstorm had flooded downtown last April? All Miles was asking for was a few seconds to mop up a bully.

floosh

The latch on one of the stalls slid back. Miles held his breath, wondering who was inside. The way his luck had turned, it was probably some new bully he hadn't met yet. Just what he needed.

The flusher stepped out of the stall, and Miles whispered a silent prayer of thanks. It was only the kid from detention—the one with the overlarge glasses and too-short pants. Clearly, he wasn't a threat to anyone. In fact, he was looking at Miles with complete awe. Honest-to-goodness awe, like he really was impressed by what he saw.

"Wow." The kid gaped, adjusting the strap on his shoulder bag. "Awesome cape."

Miles checked his reflection in the mirror, wondering if the cape had started working. Nope. He waited for the kid to yell "Gotcha!" and bust out laughing, but he kept looking Miles over appreciatively.

Miles couldn't take the awkward silence any

longer. "You really think so?" he asked.

"Totally," the kid gushed. "Best replica Gilded cape I've ever seen." He washed his hands at the sink and then turned to Miles. "Where'd you buy it?"

"I—"

"Right," the kid interrupted, as though he already knew the answer to his question. "There aren't any capes this nice on the market. I've looked. So you made it yourself? I've made my own tons of times. You know what the hardest part is?"

"I—"

"Of course you know. Duh. It's the stitching. Everybody forgets Gilded's costume doesn't have any stitching. I mean, it's not like I've been that close to him or anything—I've never even seen him in person—but I've studied enough photos and TV footage to know. I have a theory that it's made from some crazy material that doesn't need stitches. Can I touch it?"

"I—"

The kid snatched up the corner of the cape and rubbed it between his fingers, raising it to his glasses for closer inspection. "Is this satin? No. It isn't satin. Silk? What'd it cost you per foot?"

Miles had never seen anyone so excited. It was like the kid was experiencing Christmas, his birthday, and the last day of school all at the same time. Miles had not the foggiest clue how to answer any of the questions, so he steered the conversation in another direction. "Detention. You were the kid with the comic book."

The kid let go of the cape and grinned. "*Gilded Age* number 452. Mr. Constant caught me reading it during class. What's the big deal? I'd already taught myself the day's lesson." The kid shrugged. "Oh, well. Coach Lineman runs a quiet ship. Great reading environment. What's your name anyway?"

"Miles."

The kid jutted out a hand. "Henry Matte. I'm pleased to make your acquaintance, Miles."

Pleased to make your acquaintance? Did he think he was applying for a job?

Miles shook the kid's hand. "Right. Same here." Miles tried to muster some enthusiasm of his own, but it wasn't easy, given the fact he was hiding in a bathroom and wearing a cape on the fritz. "So . . . I guess you're a pretty big Gilded fan," he offered.

"Try *the* biggest. I know everything there is to know about the Golden Great. Ask me something. Go on. Anything. I'll know the answer."

Come to think of it, maybe Miles had a job opening after all. "Henry?" he said, smiling.

Henry narrowed his eyes and pressed his lips together, preparing himself for Miles's toughest bit of Gilded trivia. "Shoot," he dared.

"What are you doing this afternoon?"

MAYBE IT WAS RUDE FOR MILES TO INVITE HIMSELF over to Henry's house after school, but he didn't have much choice. He needed answers about the cape, and Henry was his best way of getting them. Even if Henry turned out not to be the walking Gilded-pedia he claimed to be, there was no doubt he knew more than Miles. Gilded's costume didn't have any stitching? Who noticed things like that? Miles had spent more time with the Gilded cape than anyone—well, anyone except the old man who gave it to him—and the thought of checking the stitching never crossed his mind. He just hoped Henry's knowledge extended to more than tailoring.

As they walked to Henry's, Miles kept looking around for the Jammer and his herd in case they wanted to finish their earlier conversation. If Henry worried about such things, it didn't show.

"You don't have any of that fabric left, do you?" he asked. "Where'd you buy it, anyway? I bet it was a special order. Ever notice how the real Gilded cape never shows any damage? I know. Right? Fires, gunfights, you name it. Can you imagine what fabric like that would mean for the poor? A single pair of pants would last forever!" Henry went on and on, lost in his one-man question-and-answer session.

When they turned the corner into Henry's neighborhood, Miles stopped cold. He gazed up at the entrance monolith, a huge manmade waterfall cascading across a waterwheel. The wheel spun lazily in the sun, dipping in and out of a crystal-clear pool that was scattered with enough loose change to pay a month's rent at the Taylor household. At the base of the monolith, wrought iron bent into cursive lettering spelled out the subdivision's name: ESTATES AT OAK GLEN.

"You live *here*?" Miles gasped.

Henry walked a few more steps before noticing Miles was no longer beside him. He broke off his Gilded reverie and turned around. "You say something?"

"You live here?" Miles repeated. "This is the Christmas neighborhood."

Henry arched an eyebrow. "Pardon?"

"This is where the houses go crazy with the lights and animatronic snowmen." Everyone knew about this neighborhood. It was a regular December feature in the local news. While some people paid by the carload for the privilege of inching through a traffic jam to see the lights at parks or botanical gardens, local families knew they could get better holiday displays for free right here. "Didn't one of the roofs have a life-sized Santa sleigh with all nine reindeer a couple of years ago?"

"Oh, that." Henry shrugged. "Sure. Mr. Snollygoster had to file a permit to install the fog machine."

Coming from anyone else, Henry's nonchalance would've rang false, like he was trying to act humble when really he was bragging. Miles had hung around the mall enough—seen enough Southern belles with their big diamonds and cooing accents—to spot a phony. But Henry struck Miles as the type of kid who honestly didn't realize how much money his parents had to earn to live in a neighborhood with the word "estates" in the title. Henry was an odd duck, but he was innocent. He didn't seem pretentious or judgmental. Miles liked him.

Miles was a long way from Cedar Lake Apartments, but he didn't realize how long until he saw the houses up close. Impressive as they were when lit up at night, they were even more impressive in the daytime. Some had white columns out front, others wraparound porches with fireplaces overlooking infinity pools. One had a barn-shaped garage topped with a copper roof and a rooster weathervane. As if there were any live-stock inside. More like Porsches and Cadillacs.

Then there were the yards. Great green swaths sep-arated the houses from one another by enough space to drop another house in between. Brick driveways stretched for fifty yards or more.

"How do you trick-or-treat in a place like this?" Miles wondered.

"Golf carts," Henry replied matter-of-factly.

Tired of walking, Miles wanted to ask Henry to fetch one of those golf carts and come back for him.

At last they reached the Matte home. The massive structure's three levels sat atop an exposed basement with its own parking area and side entry. Walking up the driveway, Miles admired the stacked stone facade and the two-tiered porch supported by thick, wooden beams. The front yard was large enough to include a pond—Miles had never known anyone who owned a body of water—complete with a paddleboat moored to a fishing dock. Everything was situated behind a copse of oak trees whose leaves were just beginning to fall. Miles wasn't sure if the trees were intended to offer privacy, but a flagpole would've had an easier time trying to hide a hippopotamus.

Henry slid his key into the doorknob, pushed the door inward, and stepped aside. "After you," he said, gesturing with a sweeping hand.

Miles crossed the threshold and caught his breath. He wouldn't have believed it was possible, but the house actually looked bigger on the inside. A line of floor-to-ceiling windows looked out onto the backyard, which sloped gently downward before disappearing into a forest of dogwoods and pines. Between the foyer and the windows was a great room decorated in leather furniture and floored with enough polished hardwood to scrimmage a roller derby team.

Everything was . . . immaculate. That was the word. Immaculate. There wasn't a speck of dust or trace of dirt to be found, not even the red Georgia clay that was the bane of clean houses everywhere. And everything matched, too, the chairs and sofa complementing the lamps and wall hangings. It was like stepping into the cover of one of those interior design magazines his mom used to leave lying around the house. Miles thought he heard angels singing.

"What do your parents do?" he asked.

"Dad's an engineer, which is a fancy way of saying he builds stuff. Mom does a bunch of volunteer work. I think she's at the food bank today. What about yours?"

Miles shifted his feet. "My dad works in construction, too. My mom is . . ." He searched for the right word. "Gone."

Henry's face dropped. "Oh. Sorry. I didn't know."

Miles could tell from the way Henry said it that he thought Miles's mom had died. Miles didn't see a need to correct him. It was better than explaining that she'd decided not to hang around.

Henry perked up suddenly. "So, you ready to see the

Gilded Cage?" Henry's hands shot up, and he wiggled his fingers as though he'd uttered some magic phrase. It wasn't a question so much as an announcement.

"Is that where you keep your dogs?" Miles cringed. "You didn't name your dog Gilded, did you?" Miles imagined a fluffy Pomeranian with a tiny golden cape.

"I would if I had a dog. I'd train it to fight crime, too." Henry's voice trailed off as he pondered the possibilities. Then he shook his head, snapping himself out of his daydream. "The Gilded Cage is what I call my bedroom. It's my headquarters. My secret lair."

"But I thought a gilded cage was a bad thing. A prison that you don't realize is a prison."

Henry huffed. "I'd like to see you come up with a cool hideout name that somehow incorporates 'gilded.' Do you want to see it, or not?"

"Sounds awesome. Lead the way."

They climbed the curved staircase up to the third-story landing, where there stood a single closed door. A sign taped to the door read, PRIVATE.

Henry grinned. "When Dad helped the architect design the house, he planned for this to be his den. I convinced him it'd make a better ... *Fortress of Gilded-tude!*" He punctuated the declaration with another bout of dancing fingers. Seeing the new name elicit no response from Miles, he dropped his hands and sighed. "You're right. Too derivative. Just come on."

If the immaculateness of the rest of the house was a cause for angels to sing, then the condition of Henry's bedroom would surely make them weep. Newspaper clippings, computer printouts, and back issues of *Gilded Age* were strewn everywhere. The room was a mishmash of odds and ends—screwdrivers and other hand tools mixed in with swatches of gold fabric and knockoff Gilded merchandise. Dirty laundry covered the floor. Miles stood frozen in the room's only clean spot, a half circle of carpet that had been swept bare by the opening of the door.

"You don't have friends over very often, do you?" Miles asked.

"Friends are overrated. I have interests. If people aren't as enthusiastic about them as I am, then so be it."

Henry spoke without an ounce of resentment. While every other kid at Chapman—Miles included—judged themselves by their friend count, Henry didn't seem to care. How someone who looked like the poster child for a teen makeover show could be so confident was beyond Miles's comprehension. But he admired it.

"Have a seat," Henry beckoned. "I'll show you where I do all my work."

Sit where? And what kind of work could he be doing in here—growing mold? Then Miles realized the room wasn't full of just junk. It held a lot of equipment, too. A laptop was buried under the papers on the desk.

The coatrack by the window was actually a telescope, and from the size of it, probably an expensive one. What appeared to be a trucker's CB radio sat on the nightstand. Miles thought he spied a metal detector next to some doodad that looked like a toy gun, but with a mini satellite dish on the end of the barrel.

A map of the greater Atlanta area had been taped to the far wall, and hundreds of dots had been drawn on it with red marker. Miles stepped into the room for a closer look.

squish

Miles lifted his shoe to find the sole smeared with purple ooze. "Sorry," he offered.

"My jelly doughnut!" Henry said cheerily. "I was looking for that!"

"Glad to help." Miles picked up a paper towel from the floor and cleaned his shoe. He nodded at the map. "What's that?"

Henry concentrated on the myriad red dots. "All the known Gilded sightings from the past two years. If I collect enough data on his response time to emergencies, I might be able to track him back to his hideout." Henry furrowed his brow. "The calculations would be easier if I knew his maximum airspeed, but no one has been able to clock him."

"So . . ." Miles acted innocent. "You said I could ask you anything about Gilded. That offer still good?"

"You bet! Just let me check something first." Henry rifled through the papers on the desk until his hand came out holding a remote control. He pointed it at the flat-screen TV sitting on a stand and turned the set on. A local news anchorwoman filled the screen.

"—awaiting a statement from the president, which we'll bring to you live as soon as it begins." The anchorwoman's makeup couldn't hide how flustered she was, like the slightest sound would send her diving under the news desk. "Meanwhile, emergency teams continue to search the rubble at the Atlanta parking garage that was the site of what appears to be humanity's first confirmed contact with extraterrestrial life."

The picture changed to an aerial shot of Miles's dad's work site. The hole in the upper deck was larger than Miles had imagined, and with the camera looking down into it, he could see a camouflage tarp draped over the pile of rubble at the bottom. Soldiers formed a perimeter around the structure, holding the news vans and civilian gawkers at bay.

The anchorwoman's voice continued over the video. "Authorities have been unable to identify the body of an elderly man found at the scene. Miraculously, he was the only casualty of yesterday's events."

Henry sat at the foot of the bed, watching the screen intently. "Crazy, right?"

"You could say that." Miles tried playing it cool, but

it was a good thing Henry was fixated on the TV.

Henry's head snapped around. "Aliens!" he blurted. "You know how long I've been saying we aren't alone in the universe? I'd like to see the haters deny it now. Did you notice how none of the teachers mentioned it? Bet they had an emergency staff meeting before school to make sure everyone knew not to talk about it. Like the whole world doesn't already know. I mean, haven't they heard of the Information Age?" Henry babbled excitedly, like the appearance of the alien somehow wasn't utterly terrifying.

The anchorwoman reappeared. "We'll be covering the . . . attack throughout the evening, but now let's go to a developing story." She looked grateful to have some garden-variety bad news to report. "Two armed suspects have robbed a gas station and fled in a vehicle belonging to one of the customers. Police believe the woman who owns the vehicle is being held hostage, and they're now pursuing the suspects on Interstate 20. Steve Voyeur in our traffic chopper has a bird's-eye view of the chase in progress. Steve, what do you see?"

"Here we go!" Henry checked his wristwatch. "Incident reported at four thirty-two and eighteen seconds." He turned to Miles, grinning from ear to ear. "Live Gilded footage. This is going to be great!"

THE TV SCREEN WAS FILLED WITH AN AERIAL SHOT OF

a red SUV swerving through traffic on the interstate. A pair of police cruisers was trying their best to catch up. Steve Voyeur chattered breathlessly, his words keeping pace with the action.

"This is a dangerous situation, viewers. The suspects are fleeing westbound at high speeds during the busy afternoon drive time."

The SUV darted across two lanes and nearly forced a bus into the guardrail.

"That was a close one!" Voyeur exclaimed. He sounded like an announcer calling a race at Atlanta Motor Speedway.

Henry's toes tapped with anticipation. If he leaned any closer to the TV, he was going to topple forward into it. "Can you believe these guys? Major crimes are still attempted in Atlanta, but Gilded never lets them succeed. Why don't the crooks pull up stakes and move to another city, you know? But I guess if they had any sense, they wouldn't be crooks to begin with."

If there had been butterflies fluttering in Miles's stomach when he thought about helping Mrs. Collins, now there were great blue herons. Taking on a mean husband was one thing. Going head-to-head against a stickup team armed with guns and a three-ton SUV was far more dangerous.

This was Miles's first real test. The city was waiting.

"Where's your bathroom?" Miles asked weakly.

"Now?" Henry gasped. "This is *live*. Using an *actual* video camera. Most of the Gilded footage out there was taken with a phone. Pure amateur hour." He pointed at Miles's feet but kept his eyes focused on the car chase. "You stay right there. I'm not letting you miss a second of this."

Miles considered making a run for it, but to where? By the time he found a safe place to put on the cape, the chase could've ended in a crash or a shootout or who knows what else. The robbers had a hostage. There wasn't a moment to lose.

Miles crept over to the window, making sure Henry didn't see. He undid the center latch and swung the double panes wide, letting in a fresh autumn breeze. He leaned out and saw it was a good thirty feet down at least. *Cape, don't fail me now.*

On the TV, the traffic grew heavier, but the SUV only

sped faster. The man in the passenger seat waved his gun like a maniac, scaring the other drivers off the road.

Henry glanced at his watch and frowned. "Forty-five seconds. What's taking him so long? Gilded's response time to crimes in progress is usually faster than this."

Miles pulled open his backpack and slid out the cape. It hummed, which was hopefully a sign that everything was back in working order.

And then Miles got scared. Really scared.

How many other anxious sets of eyes were glued to their TVs right now? Thousands? Millions? If Gilded didn't stop those robbers before they hurt someone, the whole world would know.

Miles wasn't worried about what people might think of him. No one knew he was the new Gilded. If he screwed up, though, it'd put a black mark on Gilded's stellar record.

Gilded wasn't just a superhero. He was an ideal. An umbrella in a rainstorm. A blanket on a winter night. He made people feel safe and secure. If his reputation were somehow tarnished, who would they put their trust in?

With the cape across his shoulders, Miles brought the clasp halves closer. He closed his eyes and breathed a prayer. "Please work. And don't let me suck."

"Shots fired!" Steve Voyeur shouted. "One of the robbers is—

WAIT. *YOU KNOW MY* NAME?

YEAH.

AND I NEED YOUR HELP.

MILES, YOU REALLY HAVE TO SEE THIS!

YOU WANT A DRINK? SOMETHING TO EAT? DO YOU EAT?

I'VE KEPT TABS ON YOU MY WHOLE LIFE. I'VE GOT MAPS, CHARTS, GRAPHS--

I'M GOING TO SHOW YOU SOMETHING.

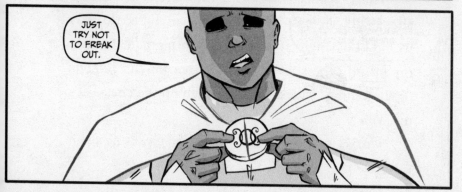

JUST TRY NOT TO FREAK OUT.

Miles felt the power leave him, and he went from towering over Henry to looking him dead in the eye. Holding the pieces of the clasp in his hands, he couldn't shake the feeling that he'd made a terrible, irreversible mistake. The original Gilded had warned Miles not to let anyone know his true identity. Ever. Miles didn't even make it twenty-four hours.

All Miles had wanted was to get a few answers from Henry. Now he'd blown the whole thing. *Nice going, genius.*

Henry's excitement morphed into confusion. Or it could've been disappointment. Either one would be completely understandable. "W-what the . . ." he stammered.

"I know it's weird, but—"

"You've got *shape-shifting* powers!" Henry exclaimed. "That makes total sense. It explains why in issue 371 of *Gilded Age* the arms dealer didn't know you were in the warehouse. Did you make yourself look like a sports car?"

"Huh?" It was Miles's turn to be confused. "I can't shape-shift. At least I don't think I can. If I could, why would I be hanging out in the seventh grade? I'd turn myself into the starting quarterback for the Falcons or something." Miles patted himself on the chest. "It's me. Miles."

Henry glanced around, like he was waiting for a

hidden camera crew to crawl out from under the bed and shout, "Gotcha! You're on *Prank TV*!" Then he perked up and snapped his fingers. "I get it. You don't age, right? You're a thousand years old or something. Pretty awesome. Of course, that means you'll be stuck in seventh grade for eternity." He frowned. "Less awesome."

Miles rubbed his forehead and sighed. "No. I was eleven last year, and next year I'll be thirteen. I'm not immortal, and I can't transform into a Corvette." He slid the cape off his shoulders and held it forward. "I don't have superpowers. The cape does."

Henry wasn't buying it. He fish-hooked an eyebrow and crossed his arms. "If you're twelve, then how have you been around since 1956?"

Miles threw his hands up in frustration. "I haven't been! That was another guy."

On the TV, the anchorwoman had gone back to covering the previous day's attack, and a news crew that had found a way inside the parking garage was filming the rubble. Miles walked over to the screen.

"You remember the old man they said died in the attack yesterday? He was the real Gilded. I was at the garage with my dad when Gilded and the lizard-monster—which, by the way, you wouldn't be so jazzed to learn was real if you'd seen it up close—crashed through the roof. The old guy killed the alien, but . . . he said it was his time to go. I guess he didn't want to do it anymore. Anyway, he gave me the cape before he died. He said I have to be the hero now."

Miles knew he sounded like a lunatic. Heck, he hardly believed it himself, and he was living it. What was a kid he'd met only a few hours ago supposed to think?

The news crew ran up to the military guy with the craggy face and the bottle-brush mustache. He'd no doubt been working long nights, but he didn't look the least bit tired. He looked like a man on a mission.

A reporter pushed a microphone in his face. "General Breckenridge, why have you cordoned off the area? What are you hiding?"

The General didn't say anything, but his tight-lipped expression and steel-gray eyes spoke a thousand words. One of his large hands reached for the camera, and the screen went black.

Miles turned off the set. "I know it sounds nuts, but you have to believe me."

"I hardly know you," Henry said skeptically. "Suppose the old man on the news was Gilded all this time, like you say. Then he must've kept one heck of a secret identity to make sure nobody found out the truth, which is too bad because he pretty much deserves to be honored with the biggest state funeral ever. Yet here you are, blabbing everything to me on day one. Why?"

"I probably shouldn't be," Miles said softly. "It's just that . . ." His shoulders dropped. "I don't know what else to do."

Miles wasn't the smartest kid, but he was smart enough to know what he didn't know, and he definitely didn't know how to be a superhero. He took pride in being a good judge of character, though. The same instinct that had warned him on the first day of school that Craig Logg was no good (granted, you didn't need to be a detective to figure that one out) was now telling him that Henry could be trusted. Miles believed it in his bones.

"Will you help me?" Miles wondered if he sounded as desperate as he felt.

"You lifted an SUV over your head on network TV!" Henry shouted in exasperation. "What do you need me for?"

"Because you know Gilded's cape doesn't have stitching. And you have a map of all his sightings from the past two years. And you have"—Miles picked up the toy gun with the satellite dish on the end—"whatever this is."

Miles was pleading, and he didn't try to hide it. Maybe he shouldn't have told Henry his secret, but he was glad he had. The burden of being Gilded was his, but at least now there was someone to help him carry it. He hoped.

"Please," he croaked. "Everyone is counting on me. And if there's one thing I've learned since yesterday, it's that I can't do this by myself."

There it was. The truth. Miles held his breath and waited for Henry to say something. Anything. As long as it wasn't a phone call to the press.

Henry walked over and took the satellite-dish thing from Miles's hand. "This is a parabolic microphone. You use it for—" He broke off his sentence and tossed it onto the bed. "Never mind. We'll get to that later."

Henry bowed at the waist like a gallant knight pledging himself to his king. "Henry Matte, at your service," he declared. Then he straightened up and smiled. "Tell me what I can do."

CHAPTER 9

IT WAS LIKE A RAIN BARREL HAD TIPPED OVER, THE whole story sloshing out of Miles all at once. He told Henry about the parking garage and the lizard-monster. He told him about picking up Mr. Collins with one hand. He described how unbelievable it felt to bring those armed robbers to justice. They'd been too afraid even to fire their guns.

Then Miles told him about crashing down before school, how the cape had suddenly turned off like someone had kicked the plug out of the wall. He explained that it still wasn't working when he'd confronted Craig. That was why he'd ended up humiliating himself and hiding in the bathroom like a loser.

Henry sat at his desk, calmly soaking in every detail. He must have been really interested, because for once he didn't interrupt.

When Miles finished, Henry stood and started

pacing in a circle. "Put the cape on," he commanded.

Miles draped the cape over his shoulders and tried to connect the clasp. The metal clacked against itself, but it didn't stick. "Nothing." He shrugged.

Henry stopped pacing. "What if it only works when there's an emergency? Like your neighbor being mean to his wife, or those criminals who kidnapped that lady. The cape knew it was needed, so it sprang into action."

Henry mulled his hypothesis. "No. That doesn't make sense. There's always an emergency somewhere, even if it's just somebody with a flat tire on the highway. The cape would always be on."

He paced again, studying the cape from every vantage point. "Is it possible it only works against evil?"

Before Miles could answer, Henry shook his head in disagreement with himself. "If that were the case, then it wouldn't work against natural disasters. In *Gilded Age* number 238, Gilded helped drivers stranded in an ice storm. Bad weather is one thing, but evil weather? That's stretching it. Besides, if Craig Logg isn't evil, I don't know who is."

Henry stood with his hands on his hips, tapping his foot in frustration. "This is a conundrum."

"That's what I've been telling you. It's like it has a mind of its own. How can I follow in the old Gilded's footsteps if I don't even know how the cape works?"

Miles dropped onto the bed. "Aw, what's the use?" he mumbled. "I'm not cut out to be a superhero."

"Exactly!" Henry blurted.

"Hey!" Miles shot back. "How about a little encouragement? You're supposed to be helping me."

If Henry was aware he'd offended Miles, he didn't show it. "What did you say? Before the part about you being a lousy superhero."

"About the cape having a mind of its own?"

"Yes." Henry stroked his chin. "Maybe it's not just the cape that has a mind. Maybe you do."

"'Maybe'? So on the brainpower chart, I'm just above a zombie. Thanks."

"What I mean is, maybe the cape somehow taps in to your brain. That's how it knows when you want to fly or throw a superpunch or whatever. Do you remember what you were thinking just before you crash-landed in the woods?"

"Sure. I was thinking about—" Miles stopped himself, his ears starting to burn. "Uh, I don't remember," he fibbed.

Henry crossed his arms. "You want my help or not?"

"Okay, fine." Miles looked down at his feet. "I was thinking about Josie Campobasso. About how . . . impressed she'd be when she saw I was a superhero."

Henry's mouth dropped open in shock. "*Josie Campobasso?* Aim a little higher, why don't you."

"Can we try to focus here?"

"Right." Henry coughed, stifling a chuckle. "Sorry. Okay, on your feet."

Miles stood again. Henry faced him, eyeing him like a scientist monitoring a lab rat. "Now, what happened when you went up against the armed robbers?"

"Well, they sped past me, and then I caught up, and I pulled the driver out of the car. The car was out of control, so . . ." Miles trailed off. "Do you really need the play-by-play? I thought you watched me on TV."

"That's not what I'm talking about. What went on up *here*?" Henry tapped an index finger against his temple. "What went through your mind?"

Miles had no idea what Henry was getting at. "Um . . . stuff?"

"Stuff. Good for you. I need more information, though. Try closing your eyes. Go on," he pressed.

Miles closed one eye, but kept the other trained on Henry. "Is this really necessary?"

"Trust me."

"All right, but no funny stuff." Miles closed both eyes and tried his best to relax. "I'm not in the mood."

"I wouldn't dream of it. Now, block out everything but the sound of me talking." Henry's usual rapid-fire delivery slowed, and he shifted into a soft, monotone voice. Miles had never been hypnotized, but he imagined this was how it started. If he left the Matte house with an irresistible urge to run in circles or cluck like a chicken, Henry was going to be sorry.

"Go back to before you turned into Gilded," Henry continued. "Better yet, pretend it's happening again. A pair of gun-wielding maniacs is on the loose. They've taken a defenseless nun hostage. They're speeding on the highway with total disregard for decency and traffic laws, endangering a school bus full of orphans and Girl Scouts. Do you feel anything?"

"I'm hungry for cookies."

"I said block everything out!" Henry scolded. "You're not blocking. Think of the nun praying for help from above. Think of the orphans and Girl Scouts with tears streaming down their cheeks. They're so scared. All they want is to make a positive contribution to society, but the bad guys won't let them. What is Gilded going to do about it?"

A bit over-the-top, but it worked. Miles imagined the Girl Scout troop rolling around the back of the bus, their driver trying to evade the hail of bullets unleashed by a team of nun-stealing evildoers most foul. That kind of behavior wasn't to be tolerated. Not in Atlanta. Not in Gilded's town.

The cape hummed to life. The vibrations started soft and grew stronger, like it was waking up from a nap. Miles concentrated on the power filling him. Power he'd use to protect others. To keep the city safe.

Never mind air rushing out of a balloon. It was like the balloon had been jammed with a pin. The power left the cape in a burst, snapping Miles back to his smaller self. A wave of queasiness washed over him.

"Ugh . . ." Miles groaned, trying not to teeter over.

Henry reached out a hand to steady him. "You okay? Tell me how you feel."

Miles staggered backward and plopped onto the bed. "Like that time at the county fair I ate five corn dogs and rode the Tilt-A-Whirl."

"You shrunk from six-and-a-half feet tall to under five feet in a blink. A sudden change like that would have to mess with your spatial awareness. Interesting it didn't affect you going the other way," he mused. "The cape must protect against that."

"Great. I'll stock up on antinausea meds."

"I have a better idea. Close your eyes again. This time, think about your neighbor lady. You can hear her husband yelling. She's cowering, scared of what he might do. Concentrate on wanting to help." Henry's voice became more intense, like he was narrating a commercial for a blockbuster movie. "Only Gilded can save her," he intoned. "But will he?"

An image of a frightened Mrs. Collins took shape in Miles's mind. The humming of the cape intensified, surging like a tide pushing the queasiness back out to sea.

HEY! I DON'T FEEL SICK ANYMORE.

MM-HMM. THAT'S THE CAPE TAKING OVER.

NOW CLOSE YOUR EYES ONE MORE TIME.

THINK ABOUT →SNICKER← JOSIE. IMAGINE YOU'RE FLYING AROUND AS GILDED, AND YOU SEE HER

IMAGINE WHAT YOU'D →HEH← DO.

I CAN HEAR YOU GRINNING, YOU KNOW.

OKAY, OKAY.

JUST IMAGINE WHATEVER YOU WANT.

THE IMPORTANT THING IS JOSIE ISN'T IN ANY KIND OF TROUBLE. YOU JUST WANT TO SHOW OFF.

Another balloon burst. Miles flopped backward, spreading out his arms to steady himself on the bed. Thick nausea bubbled inside him like overcooked chili. "And I'm sick again," he muttered.

"Do you see?" Henry beamed.

"No. But you're about to see my lunch, because I think I'm going to hurl."

"You're right. You do need my help. Sit up."

Miles pushed himself up. The queasiness was worse than before, the yo-yoing back and forth between Gilded and himself wreaking havoc on his insides. He reached out frantically and snatched up the closest thing to a container.

"Not my pillow!" Henry bawled.

Miles held open the pillowcase and buried his face inside. The nausea rolled upward into his chest, his throat . . .

"Braaap!" Miles let loose a mighty belch worthy of a superhero. The pillowcase billowed. He smacked his lips for a moment, making sure nothing was following the air outward. Relieved, he set the pillow back on the bed. "False alarm. That was a close one, though. I'd advise against any more experimenting for a while."

"We don't need to," Henry said. "You really haven't figured it out, have you?"

"Figured out what, that wearing the cape makes me sick? Does that mean I'm allergic to the fabric?"

"I hate to tell you this, Miles, but the cape doesn't make you feel like you have to barf. You make yourself feel that way."

Miles laid the cape across his lap. "Tell me something I don't know."

Henry picked up the cape. "Try to be a little more upbeat, will you? You're *the* superhero. All things considered, you have a lot to be happy about."

Henry pinched the clasp halves in the fingers of each hand and let the fabric drop to the floor. Even with the bright sunlight shining through the windows, the cape's glow was apparent. Whatever Miles had done to make it stop working, it was ready to go again.

Did the cape prefer Henry in some way? Miles felt a pang of jealousy.

"Think of the cape as a car," Henry explained, taking on a scholarly air. "These two pieces are the key to the ignition. When they're connected, the cape turns you into Gilded and away you go. When they separate, the cape stalls and you revert to your normal self. The question is, what causes the pieces to behave one way or the other?

"Having conducted our trials, I've concluded there can be only one answer: The clasp responds not just to your thoughts, but the specific nature of your thoughts. The cape helped you stop the robbers and save your neighbor, but not exact your revenge against Craig or impress—"

Miles's eyes narrowed.

"—er, someone." Henry snickered. "The former are examples of you using the cape to benefit others. The latter are examples of you trying to use the cape to benefit yourself. It won't let you do that.

"That explains why the old Gilded never signed autographs or posed for pictures." Henry was becoming more animated as he spoke. "He would've been using the cape to make himself famous. It's also why he didn't do product endorsements or write a tell-all book. He would've been using the cape to fatten his bank account. That old man knew using the cape for those reasons was wrong. More important, he understood the cape knew it.

"It's simple," Henry declared, handing the cape to Miles. "The cape only lets the wearer do what's right. And revenge, greed, and putting yourself above others isn't right."

"I don't know," Miles said doubtfully. "Giving Craig a beat down would benefit a lot of people. For one thing, it'd teach him to quit being such a jerk. It'd stop him from bullying other kids, too."

"Perhaps, but I doubt you had Craig's best interests—or anyone else's besides yours—in mind at the time."

"So, if I think about how I'm helping Craig be a

better person, the cape will let me punch him?"

Henry pressed his lips together in disapproval. "I'd advise against attempting that. If you're wrong, you'll turn back into yourself in front of Craig and everyone. Your secret identity will be blown. Besides, in terms of design and functionality, the cape far surpasses anything I've ever heard of. I highly doubt it can be fooled that easily."

Miles ran his hand along the cape. Did it really have a mind of its own? "Where do you suppose it came from?" he wondered aloud.

"It's hard to say. The old man could've made it. For all we know, he was some kind of genius inventor. If there's one thing the last twenty-four hours should've taught you, it's that *anything* is possible."

"So, I have superspeed and superstrength and I can fly, but I'm not allowed to take advantage of it? Where's the fun in that?"

"The fun is in you having superspeed, superstrength, and the ability to fly."

"You know what I mean."

Henry shrugged. "Don't expect me to know all the answers right away. I've only been working on this for a few minutes, but I already figured out what makes the cape turn on and off. That's a good start. We'll just have to work through the rest as we go. In the meantime, try to remember that doing the right thing is its own reward. Your powers aren't meant to be used for enjoyment or personal gain. They're not supposed to help you impress girls. That isn't the hero's way. So keep your thoughts, you know, pure."

A singsong voice called from downstairs. "Henry! I'm home!"

Henry's eyes went wide with fright. "My mom! You have to get out of here!" He tossed the cape to Miles, then gathered up Miles's backpack.

"What's the big deal?" Miles asked, as he slid the cape inside his pack. "She volunteers for charity. How bad can she be?"

"She's not bad at all. She's great. But she's a little too curious. If she finds you here, she'll start in with the twenty questions. She'll want to know everything there is to know about you. It won't take her long to figure out you've got something to hide."

"Please," Miles scoffed. "I know how to give a grown-up the slip."

"Hen-ry! Where are you?"

"You don't understand. She can sniff out the truth better than a polygraph machine. I've had twelve years of practice dealing with her, but you won't stand a chance." Henry shoved Miles toward the window.

"We're three stories up!" Miles shrieked.

"Shh! There's a trellis you can climb down. Just try not to crush Mom's hydrangeas."

Henry shoved Miles through the window, barely giving him a chance to grab on to the trellis. Miles started down, then stopped and called back up.

"Wait! What should I do next? You have to help me figure this stuff out!"

"Meet me at school on Monday before first bell. I'll take care of everything. Now go!"

Henry closed the window and was gone, leaving Miles dangling from a trellis thirty feet above the ground.

CHAPTER 10

MILES SOMEHOW MADE IT TO THE GROUND WITHOUT falling and breaking his neck. He was tiptoeing his way through Mrs. Matte's flower beds when a stack of comic books showered down on him.

Miles looked up to see Henry hanging out his window.

"Homework!" Henry called in a hushed tone. "And don't worry! Your secret is safe with me!" Then he shut the window again.

Miles gathered the comic books from where they'd landed among the shrubs and flowers. There were at least a dozen of them, all back issues of *Gilded Age*, of course. He might've spied a stepped-on hydrangea or two, but he couldn't be sure the offending foot belonged to him. That was his story anyway, and he was sticking to it. He made his getaway, strolling across the lawn as calmly as he could muster.

It would've been nice to fly home, but if Henry's

theory was correct, the cape didn't work like that. Ease of commute wasn't exactly a selfless desire. Miles secretly hoped for a minor emergency of some sort, something that would bring him closer to his apartment. A cat stuck in a tree or an old lady tottering across the street would be nice, but no such luck. So he hoofed it instead, and by the time he turned into the parking lot at Cedar Lake Apartments, the sun was dipping low in the sky.

His dad's truck was already parked in its spot. Miles hadn't realized he'd spent so much time at Henry's. His dad wouldn't be happy about coming home to an empty apartment. Miles was supposed to either ride the afternoon bus straight home, or call his dad if he needed to be picked up. Those were the only two options. Miles needed an excuse—preferably one that would keep him from getting grounded—and he had as long as it took to walk to his front door to think of one.

There was no point in trying to sneak past his dad. Even if the apartment weren't too small to move about in unseen, Mr. Taylor would no doubt be waiting impatiently for Miles, his emotions seesawing between anger and worry. Better for Miles to announce himself and pretend nothing was amiss. That was the way to go.

"Dad?" Miles said innocently as he walked through the door. "What're you doing home so early?"

Mr. Taylor clicked off the TV and stood from the sofa. "Nice try, son," he groused. "You know darn well what time it is. Of all the days, too. The city is up in arms over this alien thing, and I don't know where my kid is. You have any idea how that feels?"

"I know." Miles bowed his head sheepishly. He'd been so wrapped up in figuring out the cape, he'd never stopped to think his dad would be fretting over his whereabouts. Especially in light of recent events. Henry might think the existence of aliens was an exciting discovery, but the rest of the world was scared half to death. "I'm sorry I'm late. But there's a reason, and it doesn't have anything to do with detention."

"It better be good. You know the rules, and I can't have you disobeying them whenever it suits you." Mr. Taylor crossed his arms and narrowed his eyes skeptically. "So let's hear it."

"I made a friend."

Mr. Taylor raised an eyebrow. "No kidding?"

Miles couldn't help feeling a little offended. Was it that hard to believe someone would want to hang out with him? Sure, it might've been the cape Henry wanted to hang out with, but Miles had been there, too. They *had* hung out together. "No, Dad. I'm not kidding."

Mr. Taylor's face lit up. "That's great! Who is it? Are they in one of your classes? How'd you meet?"

"Jeez, we aren't dating or anything. He's just some kid. His name is Henry. I know him from detention, as a matter of fact."

"Whoa now," Mr. Taylor said alarmingly, holding his palms forward. "I'm all for you making friends, but not if it means falling in with the wrong crowd. What was he in for?"

"'What was he in for?' It's detention, not prison. And not everyone in there is from the 'wrong crowd.' He got caught reading comic books in class or something."

"You can get in trouble for that?" Mr. Taylor scratched his head. "All right, then. That doesn't sound so bad." He slid back a chair and sat at the tiny dinette table tucked into the corner of the kitchen. It was just big enough to fit two people and no more, but two was all they needed. "So what'd you guys do?"

Miles rattled off a made-up list of all the things he and Henry had done after school. They played video games. They watched TV. They shot hoops in the driveway and drank Cokes and talked about professional wrestling. You know, guy stuff.

Mr. Taylor nodded approvingly. Miles could tell he was so caught up in the details, he'd forgotten all about Miles being late. It didn't seem to occur to him that everything Miles had said was completely false. What was Miles supposed to say, that Henry was an übergeek who was helping him crack the mysteries of the Gilded cape? *Oh, and by the way, Dad, that was me you saw stopping those gun-crazy criminals on the news.* No, the truth was out of the question.

When Miles had finished recounting his fictional afternoon, Mr. Taylor sat back in his chair and beamed with satisfaction. "See there? I told you things would get better."

He bounded from his chair and into the kitchen. "This calls for a celebration. I owe you hot dogs, and I mean to deliver." He pulled a frying pan from the cupboard and clicked on the electric stove. "Good thing I picked up some fresh buns."

Mr. Taylor was typically a microwave chef, and Miles couldn't remember the last time his dad had used the stovetop. As it heated up, the kitchen filled with the acrid stench of dust being singed off the burner. Mr. Taylor didn't seem to notice. He whistled cheerily as he sliced open the package of hot dogs and drained the water into the sink. Never mind the harsh fluorescent glare of the overhead light reflecting off the Formica cabinets. He looked as happy as a man grilling out at Lake Lanier.

The phone rang. Not Mr. Taylor's company cell phone, which would've meant someone with a work-related question, or maybe that Miles's grandparents were checking in. It was the house phone. Mr. Taylor had given out the number only one time. In fact, Miles suspected his dad had activated the house phone solely to receive calls from one person and one person alone.

Mr. Taylor watched the phone as it rang a second time. And a third. He dropped a pair of hot dogs into the pan with a frown. "Go on and answer it, son."

Miles lifted the phone, cutting off its digital chirp midring. "Hello?"

"Hi, sweetheart!" a voice answered sunnily.

"Hi, Mom."

Between the showdown with the gunmen and the experiments with Henry, Miles had forgotten today was Friday, the day his mom called for her weekly conversation. She said she preferred to call on Fridays, so she could hear all about Miles's week. Miles wondered if it was because she didn't care enough to talk to him Saturday through Thursday. Why else would you go from seeing your kid every day to speaking to him on the phone once every seven?

"How was your week at school?"

The frying hot dogs sizzled and spat noisily. Mr. Taylor rattled the pan against the stovetop, rolling the hot dogs around to prevent them from burning. Miles took the phone around the corner, where it was quieter.

"Great. I'm totally the most popular kid there. The

football coach is trying to get me to try out for quarterback, but I haven't decided if I want the hassle." What was the point of being honest? If he told his mom how miserable school was, she'd only try to apologize. The last thing in the world Miles wanted from her was an apology. *Sorry I ruined your life when I ran off with another guy. I didn't see that coming. My bad.*

"That's wonderful, sweetheart! My little all-star!" Was she faking it the same way Miles was, or was she really clueless enough to think her son had what it took to play quarterback? Miles had never thrown a spiral in his life. "Football is very popular down here, you know. Jack has season tickets to the Dolphins. Box seats. We'll see a game when you come down. I know Jack would love to meet you."

Was Miles missing something? She was talking as though they'd already made plans for Miles to visit, even though she'd never actually invited him. It reminded him of how she used to buy lottery tickets and talk about all the ways she was going to spend her millions, as if winning was a foregone conclusion.

Not that Miles wanted an invitation. A football game in Florida with his mom and her new boyfriend? He'd rather spend a week having his teeth drilled.

"So, what else is new, sweetheart?"

"Not much."

"Oh, come on. Surely there must be *something*

new. Don't hold out on me. I'm your mother."

It was the way she said it. Like the role actually meant something to her. Miles couldn't take it anymore.

"We got invaded by aliens yesterday," he snapped. "Maybe you didn't hear about that all the way down in Florida, but it's pretty big news where you used to live."

The phone went quiet, and Miles knew he'd crossed the line.

"Of course I heard about that," Miles's mom said. "It's just . . . you're only twelve. I don't want you having to worry about those things."

"What does age have to do with it? That lizard-monster didn't look like he came to check IDs."

The phone went quiet again. Then Miles's mom broke the silence with one perfectly enunciated word. "What?"

"I said the lizard-monster didn't look—"

Miles cut himself off. Whoops. In his frustration, he'd revealed too much. The cat wasn't just out of the bag; it was racing around the room and clawing at the furniture.

"How do you know it looked like a lizard?" Miles's mom caught her breath. "Oh, my God." Her voice quavered. "You were *there*?"

Miles could almost hear her jaw hitting the floor.

He didn't have to see her to know her concern was expressing itself as exasperation. Like the time when he was ten, and she'd caught him poking a stick at a copperhead snake while his dad, oblivious to his son's activities, trimmed the hedges not twenty feet away. This was sort of the same thing, if that snake had been capable of leveling a city block.

"No, Mom," Miles said, trying to recover. "I, um, heard about it, is all. This kid . . . His mom works in the city . . . She's a—"

"Please, tell the truth. What were you doing downtown on a school night? Were you with your father? He took you to one of his job sites, didn't he? How many times have I told him I don't want you going to those places? All those machines driving around, and rusted nails sticking out of every other board. It's no place for a child to be."

"I'm not a child, Mom!" Miles shouldn't have raised his voice, but he couldn't help it. She was acting like he was still in pull-ups. He could take care of himself. Thanks to her and Jack the season-ticket holder, he pretty much had to. And with the Gilded cape, he'd be taking care of everyone else now, too. If she only knew the amazing things he could do.

"You *are* a child. You're *my* child. And I love you."

There it was. The words struck him like a bowling ball to the gut. He wanted to be angry with her for leaving, for making him move and change schools and start his life over from scratch. It'd be so much easier, if he didn't know she still loved him.

And if he didn't love her back. He wanted to tell her, to say those three little words that always made things better. But they were lodged in his throat, a lump he couldn't quite cough out, no matter how badly he wanted to breathe easy again. Instead there was the cold, barely audible crackle of a phone line waiting for a voice to fill the void.

Finally, Miles's mom spoke. "This isn't your fault," she said. "Could you please put your father on the phone?"

"Okay." Miles sighed. "Bye." *I love you, too, Mom.*

Miles turned back into the kitchen and held out the phone. "She wants to talk to you."

Mr. Taylor's shoulders sagged. He grabbed the phone without making eye contact and headed for the living room. "Don't let the dogs burn."

Miles took his dad's spot at the stove. The hot dogs curled in their blistering, browning skins. Over the sizzling and popping, he heard his dad's voice carrying in from the living room.

"Hey, Eve.

"No, it wasn't like that.

"Simmer down, will you?"

Miles could only eavesdrop on one side of the

conversation, but he didn't need to hear both sides to know what his mom was saying: She was blaming her ex-husband for putting their son in danger.

"Aw, the kid likes going to the job sites."

Miles had heard his parents argue many times, even more so over the past few years. Their disagreements always started out the same, with his dad downplaying the issue. No matter what it was, he'd say it was—

"—no big deal. It was after hours. It wasn't like the crew was in full swing."

Mr. Taylor's attempts to defuse the situation never worked, though. His soothing Southern drawl only goaded Miles's mom on, like she was spoiling for a fight and wasn't going to take no for an answer. The argument inevitably escalated until—

"For crying out loud! What was I supposed to do? I had work to finish. It's not like I can afford to give up any hours. Things are tight enough around here as it is.

"What?" Mr. Taylor boomed. "Are you *really* telling me what you would've done? I see. You would've done that from all the way down in Hollywood? Well, then, why don't you swing by the school and pick him up next time? Oh, that's right. *You can't!* What gives you the right to—hello? Hello?"

Mr. Taylor stomped into the kitchen and slammed

the phone onto its cradle. "That woman," he muttered. Then he turned to Miles. "I don't guess there's any chance you had the good sense to mind your own business during all that?"

Miles didn't answer, but he knew he didn't need to. The answer was written all over his face.

Mr. Taylor leaned against the counter and rubbed his beard. He looked tired. Spent. "Miles, when your mom and me go at each other like that, it doesn't have anything to do with you."

Nothing to do with him? The entire fight had been about him. They always were. His parents argued about his bedtime, and his grades, and his extracurricular activities (or lack thereof). Miles felt like a wire fence dividing his parents from each other, and every time they tried to get closer, they pricked themselves on the barbs. The question nagged at him—if he weren't around, would they still be married?—but he forced it to the back of his mind.

"It sure sounded like it did."

"I know it did, son. I know. But if we weren't arguing about whether or not you should be coming to work with me, we'd be arguing about something else. Somewhere along the line, your mom and me got broke. Heck, maybe we were always that way, and we were just too young to know it." Mr. Taylor pressed his lips together. "But broke as we were, your mom always said we managed to get one thing right. And that thing is you."

"If I'm so right, then why did she . . . ?" Miles's voice cracked. He couldn't say it, no matter how obvious the question was. Tears stung his eyes, and he looked away.

His dad looked away, too, and Miles wondered if he was feeling a sting in his own eyes. "If I knew that, I would've figured out a way to keep it from happening."

They stood apart, neither of them knowing what to say next.

The kitchen fire alarm changed the subject. It shrieked suddenly, and Miles and his dad nearly jumped out of their shoes.

"The dogs!" Mr. Taylor yelped.

He pushed Miles aside and yanked the frying pan off the burner, but it was too late. Smoke was already billowing from the pan. He pulled up the kitchen window and fanned the smoke out with one hand.

"Wave a towel in front of that squaller!" he hollered, trying to be heard over the deafening wail of the alarm.

Miles snatched up a dish towel and leaped onto the countertop, so he could get closer to the alarm. He waved the towel furiously, breathing in smoke and coughing it back out again. It tasted like hot dogs, if hot dogs were made of charcoal.

After a minute, the alarm fell silent. His dad dropped the pan back onto the stove, looking down at the hot dogs grimly. The tops didn't look so bad, but when he rolled them over, the undersides looked like sunbaked pavement. He prodded them with his finger, and the scorched skin flaked off.

"I'll take dibs on these," he offered. "I like mine a little crispy anyway."

Miles had been hungry a few minutes ago, but after listening to his parents fight, he'd lost his appetite. "I just remembered that Henry's mom made us sandwiches," he lied. "I didn't want to be rude, so I filled up over there. Sorry."

For a second, Miles thought his dad might force the issue, but instead he smiled weakly. "No, you don't want to be rude. A mom fixes you a sandwich, you best give thanks and eat it."

"Yeah," Miles agreed.

"Go on, then," Mr. Taylor said, nodding in the direction of the hallway. "I can tell you're itching to go to your room. You're excused."

NEVER, IN ALL HIS YEARS OF CONQUERING, HAD LORD Commander Calamity gazed upon a horde as wicked, hateful, and perfectly Unnd-trained as the one that stood before him now. There were platoons of gutting warriors wielding corkscrewed disemboweling drills. Ranks of clubbers hoisting two-handed smash-bats. Even an entire battalion of skiff-riders with halberds sharp enough to shave the fur from a boar-fly while it slumbered.

The Lord Commander had assembled the horde for a single purpose: to kill the *GGARL!* that had been located, capture its golden cape, and slaughter the inhabitants of Earth in the most Unnd-compassionate manner imaginable.

Make that three single purposes. The Lord Commander has always been an overachiever.

All was silent. The Lord Commander stood tall on the balcony outside his great chamber with his best battle blade, Crymaker the Mutilator, at his side. He knew the horde was waiting for him to deliver a rousing speech, but he wasn't sure he'd made them wait long enough. No doubt they were already quite disgruntled, but they were Unnd warriors. The more disgruntled they were, the better.

The Lord Commander glanced at his quivering servant, who clutched a timepiece in one trembling hand.

"Well?" the Lord Commander asked.

The servant shivered like a leaf with a high fever. "Y-you've made them s-stand in full armor in the scorching h-heat for twice as long as standard Unnd etiquette d-dictates, Lord Commander. A f-fitting decision for a l-leader twice as horrible as any other."

The Lord Commander puffed out his chest. "Thank you."

"My p-pleasure."

The moment had at last arrived. The Lord Commander cleared his throat, dislodging an unruly glob of mucus. He swallowed it down for luck.

"*Unnd horde!*" he bellowed. "*Hear my—*"

"Oh, Oogie!" a shrill voice interrupted. "Don't start without me, Oogie!"

The Lord Commander winced. He turned to see a rotund Unnd matron hurrying toward him from inside his great chamber. She wore a jangle-beast pelt and iron tusk rings. She held a large gourd in one hand.

"Mother . . ." He groaned. "I was about to give my most Unnd-inspiring speech yet."

"Not if I'm not there to hear it, Oogie!"

The Lord Commander glanced at those around him warily. "Mother," he whispered, "please don't call me 'Oogie' in front of the other warriors."

"Oogalus Berbert Calamity!" Mother Calamity huffed. "I carried you in my belly sac for eleven moon cycles! I will call you what I please!"

The Lord Commander lowered his eyes sheepishly. "Yes, Mother."

"Now here." Mother Calamity held forward the gourd. A murky, greenish liquid sloshed within. "I cooked you a little something for your trip."

The Lord Commander perked up. "Rodent bile soup!" he blurted excitedly. He opened the top, and a pungent odor wafted over the balcony. "Is it extra gassy?"

Mother Calamity pinched one of the Lord Commander's tusks. "Just how you like it, Oogie. Now close it up before all the fumes escape."

The Lord Commander did as he was told. He handed the sealed gourd to his servant, who looked like he was about to keel over. "My mother made this rodent bile soup for *me*," he sneered. "Don't you taste a single drop."

"Y-you have my s-solemn vow," the servant said, nodding.

"Go on and give your speech now, Oogie. I didn't put my beard in a bun for nothing."

The Lord Commander turned back to the waiting horde. *"Unnd horde! Hear my words!"* The Lord Commander paused for Unnd-dramatic effect. *"We're going to Earth. Kill everything, or I will kill you!"*

The Lord Commander's speech was finished. He waited for a resounding cheer from the horde, but none came. Perhaps they thought he was pausing again to be even more Unnd-dramatic.

"GGARL!" the Lord Commander boomed. He thrust Crymaker the Mutilator into the air and launched a mucus glob over the balcony.

"GGARL!" the horde roared in unison. They spat so many mucus globs onto the ground, Mother Calamity's clapping could barely be heard over their steaming.

The horde turned and began marching aboard the Lord Commander's battle cruiser, their boots stomping the ground in rhythm. The Lord Commander felt the balcony shaking beneath his feet, and he knew this was the horde that would bring him a golden cape at last.

"V-very Unnd-inspiring, Lord Commander," the servant said shakily. "As advertised."

"Your skill at groveling has improved greatly, servant." The Lord Commander nodded. Then he turned and yelled at one of his gathered fortress guards. "Snarlpustule!"

Snarlpustule stepped forward. "Sir!"

"See that this servant joins me aboard my battle cruiser." The Lord Commander always traveled with servants, particularly those who excelled at quivering. They were good role models for the newly conquered.

"At once, sir!" Snarlpustule hoisted the servant by the scruff of his neck and carried him from the room, nearly causing him to drop the gourd of rodent bile soup. The servant hugged the gourd tightly to his chest and whimpered.

"Oh, Oogie," Mother Calamity cooed. "You make a matron so Unnd-proud." She dabbed at her eyes with a mucus bib, then blew her snout into it. She offered the bib tearfully to the Lord Commander. "To remind you of home."

The Lord Commander took the bib. Though he would never admit it—and he would kill anyone who he even suspected had taken notice—he felt a small dampness welling at the corner of one eye. "I'll carry it with me until I return in glory."

"If you found an Unnd-nice matron of your own to settle down with, you wouldn't need to carry your mother's mucus bib, would you? That Gargonia girl is rather revolting and knobby around the—"

"Mother!"

"Fine. Run along, then."

The Lord Commander did as he was told. He ran through his great chamber and bounded down the steps of his horrible fortress with the excitement of an Unndling on his first day of bloodletting camp. He joined the last of his horde as it strode aboard his battle cruiser, and the last thing he saw as the gangplank closed behind him was his mother waving from the balcony.

He hoped there was curdle pudding waiting in the fortress cellar when he returned.

MILES NEEDED AN ESCAPE. HE DIDN'T WANT TO DWELL
on his dad or his mom or all the things he should or
shouldn't have done to keep their marriage together.
That was in the past. The very near, very painful past,
but still the past. There was nothing he could do about
any of that now.

But the future . . . There was plenty Miles could do
about the future, and he planned to do it all. He just
needed instructions.

Miles spread Henry's copies of *Gilded Age* on his
bed, wondering which to read first. He instinctively
arranged them in order by issue number and was
miffed to see they were completely out of sequence.
Oh, well. He'd fill in the missing issues later. Provided
Henry could locate them in that sty he called a bedroom.

Miles dove in. He'd never really read a comic
book before—he'd always thought they were kind of

hokey—but as he pored over the stories, he had to admit there was something engrossing about them.

In issue 265, Gilded busted up a ring of shoplifters operating out of a U-Haul stuffed with stolen cell phones and designer clothes. He made the thieves confess and then used his superspeed to return all the stolen goods to the stores they'd come from in a single afternoon.

Issue 282 told a story about Gilded taking down a gang that had set up shop in a family neighborhood. Mean as the gang was, their knives and guns and tough talk were no match for the Twenty-Four-Karat Champion.

Miles was hooked. The comic books weren't hokey at all. They were full of hope, brimming with the promise of a tomorrow that would be better than today—a message Miles was wholeheartedly onboard with, since his todays pretty much stank. He found himself becoming so invested in the stories, he kept forgetting the reason he was reading them: to learn what the cape could do.

What *he* could do. Could he really clap his hands together so hard, it'd create a tidal wave (issue 307)? Was it really possible for him to carry a mobile home on his back (issue 314)?

As he read, a warm sensation started in his chest and swelled until it seemed like his heart would burst out of his rib cage. It was an emotion he hadn't experienced in a long time. It was pride. The people were safe with the cape in Miles Taylor's hands. He would never let them down.

Miles finished every single comic book Henry had given him, and then he read them all again. He read until the late-night hours, eventually falling asleep facedown on an open copy of issue 299.

The double-page spread showed Gilded flying across a clear blue sky, his golden costume gleaming in the bright, yellow sun.

Miles's weekend went pretty much like that. He holed himself up, studying the copies of *Gilded Age* until he knew them backward and forward. He emerged every few hours for a drink or a bowl of cereal, then returned to his room before his dad could invite him to watch football. He felt guilty about not spending time with his dad, but he had the greater good to consider. There were too many questions that needed answers. He had too much to learn.

When Monday morning arrived, Miles bounded out of bed, excited for the first time in a very long time about the beginning of a new school week. He loaded the cape and comic books into his backpack and headed for the bus stop, hoping Henry had thought ahead and would bring more back issues of *Gilded*

Age to school. Miles would've called to remind him, but in the rush to escape from Henry's house, they'd forgotten to exchange phone numbers.

Miles was looking forward to seeing his new friend. He wanted to show off all the things he'd learned. Heck, maybe there was a thing or two about Gilded he could tell Henry for a change. Okay, that was probably a stretch. But Miles definitely knew his stuff now. At least he could talk to Henry and not feel completely lost.

When he stepped off the bus, Henry was waiting for him. "Where have you been?" he scolded.

It wasn't the welcome Miles had been expecting. He looked around, just to make sure Henry was talking to him. "Home?" he offered.

"DOING WHAT?" Henry screeched. He was worked up, exasperated. What had gotten into him?

"Reading up on Gilded, remember?" Miles pulled the comic books from his backpack. "There's some really great stuff in these. I totally get why you're so into them. I realize I'm not exactly unbiased, but—"

"Come with me," Henry cut in. He clamped his hand onto Miles's arm and started hauling him through the bus corral.

"Is there a problem?" Miles nearly dropped the comic books, but he recovered before they slipped from his hands. He accidentally bent one in half, but they were already so worn, he doubted Henry would notice.

Henry pulled Miles around the corner and checked to make sure they were alone. Then he wheeled on Miles.

"The whole point of reading the comics was to show you how to use the cape." Henry glared, his eyes bulging behind the thick lenses of his glasses. Miles wouldn't have thought it possible for a kid to be intimidating when his largest attribute was his eyeglass prescription, but Henry pulled it off. "So how come you didn't—oh, I don't know—*use the cape*?"

Miles was fed up. "What's with you?" he snapped. "I thought you'd be happy. I studied the comics like you said. I'm ready to go. Just point me in the direction of the nearest crisis, and I'll go to work."

Henry crossed his arms, and his eyebrows shot up, like he was waiting for Miles to connect the dots.

Miles studied Henry for a moment, and then his heart sank. "Oh no." How could he have been so stupid? "I already missed the crisis."

"Not at all." Henry's voice dripped with sarcasm. "There was that little problem with the airliner having to make a belly landing because it couldn't get its landing gear down, but I don't know that I'd classify that as a crisis. There were only ninety-seven passengers and crew members onboard, so it wasn't like the plane was *full*."

Ninety-seven people. Guilt pressed on Miles's chest like a hundred-pound dumbbell, making it hard for him to breathe. He leaned against the wall to steady himself. Ninety-seven men, women, and children gone, all because their superhero protector was too wrapped up in a stack of comic books.

Miles imagined them sobbing, their last thoughts focused on him and why he didn't save them. "Did anyone survive?" he croaked.

"They all did, but that isn't the point . . ." Henry trailed off. "You didn't hear about it?"

Miles shook his head.

Now it was Henry's turn to feel guilty. "Oh, man. Sorry. I figured you knew. Relax. Everyone's fine. The plane circled the airport for a while, waiting for you to arrive. The anchorman was sure you were going to show up. He kept saying 'any second now' over and over. It was pretty painful to watch. Luckily, the ground crew had sprayed the runway with foam just in case. It got to the point that the plane didn't have the fuel to wait any longer, so the pilot brought it down like it was landing in a bubble bath. Everyone onboard was scared, but nobody got hurt. Don't you watch the news?"

Miles exhaled deeply. He'd dodged a bullet the size of a jumbo jet. "My dad watches football on the weekends. SEC on Saturday and NFL on Sunday. I can't get near the TV." It was a lame excuse, but it was true. Of course, it was also true that Miles had never once thought to ask his dad if he could check the news, but he left that part out. Henry was miffed enough by Miles's failure. An admission like that might cause his head to explode.

"You don't have a TV in your room?" Henry asked.

"I'm not allowed."

"Internet?"

Miles shrugged.

Henry was appalled. "This is the Information Age. How do you intend to get your information?"

"I guess I hadn't thought about it," Miles said guiltily.

"Then it's a good thing I have." Henry glanced conspiratorially at the kids filling the hallway around them. "Let's find a more private place to talk."

Miles followed Henry to the end of the hallway and into an alcove outside the janitor's closet. It was a quiet, out-of-the-way part of the school he'd never known existed, but then Henry had been walking these halls far longer than he had.

Henry waited a moment to make sure no one had followed them, then reached into his shoulder bag and took out a flip-model cell phone. "You'll need this for starters."

Miles did a double take. "You're giving me your cell phone?"

"Technically, yes, but it isn't really mine. I mean, I registered it in my name, but I bought it for you. You're a superhero. You have to be reachable."

"Henry, I can't . . ." Miles couldn't bring himself to say aloud that he didn't have a cell phone for the same reason there was only one TV at the Taylor house, and no computer or Internet. His dad didn't have the money to pay for those things. What he did have was a mountain of bills sitting on the kitchen counter, a result of their household suddenly going from two incomes to one. Personal electronics probably grew on trees in the Estates at Oak Glen, but not so where Miles lived.

"It's a prepaid account, so there won't be a monthly bill. When it gets low on minutes, I'll recharge it for you." Henry pretended not to understand that Miles couldn't afford his own phone, but if there was one thing Miles had learned about Henry, he was no dummy. He was giving Miles an out, and Miles was grateful. "Besides, you won't be using it much. I'm the only one who'll have the number."

"Okay, but if nobody else has the number, how are they going to let me know when there's trouble?"

"They won't. I will." Henry showed Miles another phone, a smartphone that he must have recently gotten because it didn't have spaghetti sauce or anything on it yet. "I'll be monitoring the city with this. I've set it up to get text alerts from all the local radio and TV stations. Cable news and the Weather Channel, too. Check it out."

He passed Miles the phone, and Miles flipped through the screens. There were dozens of news apps installed, everything from ABC to *Scientific American*. There were plenty of other apps too, including a compass, a conversion calculator, and not one, but two different star charts. Unsurprisingly, they weren't in any discernible order. Miles started moving them between screens, grouping them according to subject matter.

"Stop that!" Henry snatched the phone and began putting the apps back where they were.

"I was just trying to organize them for you."

"They *are* organized," Henry huffed.

"According to what?"

"According to where I want them!" Where Henry wanted them mustn't have been all that clear even to him because it took him several tries to get the screens right. When he was finished, he showed Miles the home screen. "Anyway, as soon as something happens, I'll know. I'll text you with the problem and the location, and the rest will be up to you."

Miles noticed an icon on the screen, a golden *G* with a pair of wings sprouting from it. "What's this?"

"That's the most important news source of all. The Gilded Group."

Henry launched the app, and the phone screen was filled with information. At the top were details on Gilded's last known sighting—Friday's incident with the gunmen on I-20. At the bottom was a scrolling feed where members posted thoughts and comments about Gilded. Most of them were wondering why their hero hadn't helped the airliner with the faulty landing gear. Miles tried not to read too much of it.

"It's the main open-source information aggregator for everything Gilded related. Nine times out of ten, the members will learn of a potential crisis and post about it before any of the news outlets do, trying to predict where Gilded will show. Once Gilded has resolved it, they'll recap events and post an analysis. Remember the map on my wall? Well, you don't get that kind of data by scrolling through microfiche at the library."

"Micro-what?"

"It's not important. All you need to know is these people are our allies. I should know. I've been a Gilded Group member for four years."

All those people watching Gilded's every move. Predicting where he'll be. Expecting him to arrive. Grading his performance afterward. Miles sure hoped they were his allies.

Henry slipped the smartphone back into his bag. "Have your phone on you at all times. And remember, it's for Gilded business only. Keep the line clear."

"Got it."

"All right. We should probably get to class now." Henry started to leave the alcove, then turned back. "Almost forgot." He dug into his bag, pushing through the homework assignments and food wrappers. "Could've sworn I brought one . . . " His hand settled on something, and his face lit up. "There it is!"

Henry handed Miles a pad of paper. It was a full stack of hall passes, all of them presigned by Assistant Principal Harangue. This was contraband of the highest order. If he got caught with these, it'd mean a life sentence in detention. Miles fought the urge to toss them away like a hand grenade. "Where'd you get these?"

"I help Mr. Harangue with new student orientation. Show new transfers how to find their classes, assign them a locker, stuff like that. He gave me the pad and told me to fill one out whenever I need to be excused from class. He trusts me."

Miles had to hand it to Henry. The kid really had thought of everything. Everything except . . .

"What about PE? I won't be able keep the phone— or the cape, for that matter—within reach. What do I do about that?"

Henry stroked his chin. "That's a tough one. I'll think of something. But for now, just tell Coach Lineman you have seasonal asthma."

"Is that even a real thing?"

"Beats me," Henry said, shrugging. "But if he argues, tell him your dad is a lawyer. Now, come on. Let's not be late for first period."

CHAPTER
13

MILES HADN'T EVEN MADE IT THROUGH MORNING roll call when the phone went off for the first time. Luckily, Henry had set the phone on vibrate, so Mr. Grammar didn't hear it. But the sudden buzz in his front pocket nearly caused Miles to leap out of his chair.

vrrrrrrr

Miles clamored for the phone, his heart rate rocketing from zero to infinity in two seconds flat. Maybe everything had turned out okay with the airliner, but learning about that incident after the fact had put a serious scare into him. What would the crisis be this time? A derailed train? A bomb threat? Some unimaginable tragedy he couldn't imagine?

Miles's hand trembled, and not because the phone was vibrating again. He hid the phone under his desk and checked the screen.

Test.

Test? What could Henry's cryptic message mean? Was he saying this was going to be the first big test of Miles's abilities? Miles's thumb tapped out a hurried reply.

Where what's wrong?

An excruciating pause. Miles was breathless. The situation must be so dire, it couldn't be truncated into typical texting lingo. This wouldn't be a case of *c u l8r.*

Finally, Henry responded. *That was a test. Making sure u got the message. Will let u know if something comes up.*

Miles leaned back in his desk and closed his eyes, letting the adrenaline dissipate. He hadn't gone anywhere or done a thing, but he felt drained, like he'd just dug a new course for the Chattahoochee River.

A test. That made sense. If nothing else, they needed to be sure the phone was working correctly. If he was being honest, Miles had to admit he'd probably do the same thing, prone as he was to dotting his i's and crossing his t's. But couldn't they have tested it before school? Henry had nearly thrown him into a full-blown panic attack.

No sense dwelling on it now. Henry knew the phone was working, and all systems were go. The next text he sent would no doubt be a call to action.

Another message came through in second period, and another in third. Between third and fourth periods, the phone vibrated again, and Miles had to stop short in the hallway to dig it out of his pocket. He was nearly trampled by a gaggle of band kids trying to beat the bell.

Each time it was the same, a *vrrrrrrr* propelling Miles on an adrenaline roller coaster, only to have him read a single word: *Test*. Miles's responses ranged from a simple *Got it* to a more firm *GOT IT* and, finally, to a fed-up *GOT IT!!!* Their communications system had only been up and running for a few hours, but Henry was already becoming a nuisance. Pretty soon they truly would need a test—to make sure all the testing hadn't exhausted the phone's battery.

By lunchtime there had been five test texts, plus a sixth saying *Meet in cafeteria for recap*.

Recap? Recap what? Clearly, Miles needed to establish some ground rules, or the stress was going to turn him into the only gray-haired seventh grader at Chapman.

Miles found Henry waiting for him at the end of the line. He was bustling with energy.

"Good work on the texting. You think I should send a few more tests? Yeah, I should send a few more tests. Better make sure the phone gets a signal in all of your classes. How'd it go in PE?"

"I—"

"That's right, you don't have PE until sixth period.

I printed out your schedule from Mr. Harangue's computer." They started working their way through the lunch line, but Henry was on autopilot, answering his own questions. "That'll be the big test. Will you be in the gym? The gym is the thickest building on campus. All concrete and rebar. How thick do you think walls can be and still get a signal?"

"How would—"

"I'll have to research that." Henry dropped a peach and a banana yogurt onto his tray. "I wonder if there are any buildings we should avoid altogether. Movie theaters, supermarkets. Places like that. My mom's phone doesn't get a signal inside Target. You ever shop at Target?"

"Not too—"

"Better steer clear of it then, just to be safe."

"Henry!" Miles burst in. It was all too much. Miles hadn't used the cape a single time since he and Henry had formed their partnership, and he was already overwhelmed. He knew being Gilded was an important job, but he hadn't realized one of the requirements would be that he was on call every waking moment. And probably his sleeping moments, too.

"Can we slow down for a second? There has to be an easier way. What if I check my phone whenever I arrive someplace, and if there's no signal, I'll leave? You can count on me to do that."

"Hmph." Henry frowned. "Try telling that to the passengers who were onboard Flight 2218."

"That's not fair! I told you I couldn't get to the TV."

"All I'm saying is you need to be ready."

"Ready for what?"

"Anything." The way Henry said it, it was like he had a particular anything in mind, but he didn't want to freak Miles out. Which was good because Miles didn't think he could take being freaked out any more than he already was.

"That's why we have the phones. You'll stay on top of the news, and I'll make sure I always have the cape with me. We can't be a team if we don't trust each other to do our jobs."

Henry nodded. "You make a persuasive argument."

"Really?" Miles weighed the pros and cons of the beef stroganoff versus the teriyaki chicken. Talk about picking your poison. He opted for a slice of cheese pizza instead.

"Yeah, but don't let it go to your head." Henry slid his tray down to the cashier. "I should probably check in with the Gilded Group again."

They paid for their lunches and found two open seats at an out-of-the-way table. Henry appraised the odd assortment of food on his tray—the peach and the yogurt, a bean burrito, mashed potatoes and gravy, and chocolate milk—as though he didn't know where any of it had come from. He shrugged, tore a bite out of his burrito, and started tapping away at his phone.

Miles picked at his pizza with a plastic fork. Was this all there was to being a superhero? Cafeteria lunches and an overzealous partner who was going to drive him nuts with preparations?

In the past, Miles had never really given much thought to what life as Gilded must be like. It was a goal too unattainable to even ponder. But if he had, he would've imagined far more than this. Sure, wearing the cape was more wonderful than any feeling he'd ever had, but that was the problem: He hadn't gotten to wear it all that much. It'd been almost a week since the old man had given it to him, and he'd worn it for a total of twenty minutes max.

Because apparently—and here was the joke—the cape decided when Miles was allowed to wear it. That was the frustrating part. Famous musicians and actors and athletes lived lives filled with all kinds of perks, but they weren't as famous or extraordinary as Gilded. Doctors had private jets and houses in the Caribbean, but not even the most successful surgeon had saved as many lives as the Golden Great. Yet any of those people could fly to New York City on a moment's notice and buy an oversized slice of the pizza Miles had always heard was the best in the world. Miles was stuck eating a microwaved slab, condensation beading on its cheese like sweat. Yum.

Maybe he was being selfish. Over the last few days, he'd done something only one other person (as far as Miles knew) had done in the history of mankind: He'd been not just a hero, but a superhero. And he'd done it twice. Wouldn't most people settle for just five seconds of experiencing something so extraordinary? Why did Miles always find a way to focus on the negative?

On top of all that, he was racked with worry that he wasn't the right man for the job. He wasn't a man at all. He was twelve. What did he know about being a hero? He hadn't even made it through the first year of Cub Scouts.

Miles was plumbing new depths of despair when he saw something that lifted his spirits higher than he would've thought possible.

Josie. And she was walking right toward him.

Josie's hair was pulled back in a ponytail that bobbed playfully as she walked. Miles felt bad for the girls walking with her. Next to anyone else, they'd be knockouts. Next to Josie, they were ordinary.

Miles expected the group would pass by him on their way to the back of the cafeteria, where the upper crust always sat. But then Josie stopped at his table and turned to her friends.

"I'll catch up with you guys later," she said.

The only person more dumbstruck than the rest of the girls was Miles. Why on earth would Josie want to talk to him?

"Okaaay," one of the girls said in confusion. Then the group walked off, checking back over their shoulders to see what Josie was up to.

Miles wondered if she noticed something different about him. Something new and improved, something stronger, something—dare he think it?—heroic.

"Hi, Henry."

If Miles had whipped his head around any faster, it would've fallen off his shoulders and spun across the cafeteria floor like a top. He gawked at Henry, who didn't seem to care that the most gorgeous girl in existence was talking to him. He continued tapping at his phone, not bothering to glance up. "Hey, Josie. What's up?"

Josie wasn't put off by Henry's indifference, as though she knew him well enough to not take it personally. "My mom wanted me to tell you thanks for debugging her laptop. It's running much faster now."

Still no eye contact from Henry. "No problem. If she ever has any trouble, she can give me a call."

A call? Miles should've been focusing on Josie, soaking in every detail of her smooth skin and large, dazzling eyes. Chances were he'd never be this close to her again. But he couldn't take his eyes off Henry.

Josie's mom had his phone number? The thought of it was too surreal to put into words. It made wearing a cape and flying around the city seem as normal as a Sunday drive. The only thing that kept Miles from passing out in shock was knowing he'd end up face-down in a slice of sweaty pizza.

Miles cleared his throat, but it failed to break Henry's concentration. He cleared it again, louder.

Henry frowned as he scrolled through the Gilded Group feed. Whatever he was reading, it had a strangle-hold on his attention. "Take a drink, man. Sounds like you've got a tickle in your throat."

Miles barked again, and the sounded echoed off the cafeteria walls.

Henry looked up at him with annoyance. "You coming down with something? Have a sip of water, will you?"

Miles shifted his eyes furtively in Josie's direction.

"Oh, right!" Henry pronounced. "Sorry. Josie, this is my friend Miles Taylor. I met him in the bathroom."

Josie's eyes popped wide. It took everything Miles had to not smack Henry on the forehead.

"Miles, this is Josie Campobasso. We grew up down the street from each other. Our moms do a lot of volunteer work together."

Miles turned his head slowly, trying to act casual. When his eyes settled on Josie again, he let them linger. He'd been given permission to look at her, and he wasn't going to let the opportunity go to waste.

Josie flashed her pretty smile. "Hi."

Miles suddenly realized, to his sheer terror, he had not a clue what to say. "I go to school here," he stammered. Ugh. Who deserved a forehead smack now?

Josie cocked an eyebrow. "I kind of figured, you being in the cafeteria and all."

"Right." Miles turned to Henry, looking for backup. If Henry could get a conversation going, Miles would take it from there. He just needed a little jump start. Henry was wrapped up in the phone again, though.

Unfortunately, the worst possible person joined the conversation to fill Henry's spot.

"Hey, Camp-o-bass-o!" The Jammer sauntered over to Josie with Dude the Teammate at his side. The Jammer's lunch tray was a Noah's ark of food, piled high with two of everything on the menu. Miles supposed it took a lot of fuel to keep that mammoth body moving. "What're you doing, Camp-o-bass-o?"

Craig enunciated each syllable of Josie's last name loudly, no doubt because he thought it was devastatingly charming. Miles wanted to devastate his face.

Josie didn't seem to find it all that charming either. "I'm about to eat."

"With twerp Taylor?" Craig seemed genuinely perplexed.

Miles wanted to disappear. He'd rather be anywhere than here, made to look like a fool in front of Josie. Again. There wasn't much point to Miles being present anyway. There was absolutely nothing he could do to defend himself.

Face facts, Miles thought. *Even with the cape, you're still nothing.*

"Hey, Craig," Henry piped up.

Craig looked at Dude the Teammate and jabbed a thumb in Henry's direction. "Do I know that kid?"

"Dude." Dude the Teammate shook his head, as though the thought of someone of the Jammer's status being familiar with Henry was socially unethical.

The Jammer turned back to Henry. "What's up?"

Henry smirked. "Mouth as big as yours, you think you can cram all that food in it at the same time?"

The Jammer started forward like someone had hiked a football. "Listen here, lightweight."

Josie stepped in front of him. "Don't mind him, Craig. Why don't you find a place to sit, and I'll come join you in a minute."

Beauty calmed the savage beast. "Sure thing, Camp-o-bass-o. I'll leave just enough space next to me for you to squeeze in *real* close." The Jammer headed off across the cafeteria. "Later, twerps."

Josie wheeled on Henry. "Seriously. What's the matter with you?"

"Seriously," Miles echoed. Would the cape have helped him fend off Craig, if Henry was the one who instigated the fight? Miles wasn't sure. He had to admit it, though—Henry had guts.

Henry waved a hand, brushing aside their fears. "He touches me, Mr. Harangue will put him in detention. The Jammer ends up in detention, he misses practice. He misses practice, he has to deal with his coaches. He doesn't want that."

"That's asking Craig to do a lot of thinking before he punches you," Josie scolded. "You're lucky I was here to calm him down."

"About that . . ." Henry frowned apologetically. "You aren't really going to sit with him now, are you?"

Josie rolled her eyes. "Ugh. No way."

"Good. That's really good." Henry was back to minding his phone. "I, uh, have to step away for a second. You two get to know each other." Henry slid out of his seat and walked off, his eyes studying the screen.

Miles was abandoned, set adrift at his table in the sea of the cafeteria. He wanted to speak, but his tongue was balled into knots. Every second that went by, the closer he came to blowing the best—and probably only—chance he'd ever get to make a lasting impression on Josie. He was drowning, gasping for words. Josie tossed him a life preserver.

"Mind if I sit?"

A simple no was all Miles needed, but he couldn't muster even that.

Josie shrugged and sat across from Miles. She set a small lunch sack on the table in front of her. It was a brown-and-pink zipper bag stitched with a pattern of trees and singing birds. So she brought her lunch from home. Good for her. She was far too exceptional to settle for cafeteria dreck.

Josie arranged her lunch on the table. She hefted her ham and cheese sandwich with both hands, not minding that it hadn't been divided into more manageable quarters. She locked eyes with Miles over the top of the sandwich and took her first bite. It was nothing short of glamorous. Miles was in love.

Miles prodded his voice into action. "I'm new. Seventh grade."

"Sure. I recognize you."

Miles's heart fluttered. *She* recognized *him*. She knew he existed after all. How he wished Henry had heard that. Where had he gotten off to, anyway?

Then Josie's cheeks flushed pink, and Miles's elation evaporated. He realized a dashing appearance and winning charm weren't what had brought him to Josie's attention. It was having the soda dropped on his head, or getting slugged in the gut, or any of the countless other embarrassing moments Craig had inflicted upon him. Miles tucked his head down into his shoulders, trying to hide inside himself.

"No!" Josie blurted. "I've seen you around, is all." She was pretending she hadn't witnessed his humiliations, when he knew she had. Somehow, despite being so popular, she'd remained a nice person. She was every bit the opposite of the Jammer, and not just in the looks department.

Miles nodded. "I recognize you, too."

Josie smiled. "How do you like Chapman?"

"It's all right. I'm still figuring things out. I guess you know your way around pretty good."

Josie scanned her surroundings with a bored expression. "Too good. I've been here since the first day of sixth grade, and I've been going to school with most of these people for a lot longer than that. Some of them since pre-K. I'm ready for high school. Something different." She turned to Miles, her eyes twinkling with the promise of discovery. "Break the routine. Change things up, you know?"

"Totally," Miles said eagerly, when really he meant "not in the least bit." Routine was the only thing he could rely on. Without it, he'd be sunk. But he was talking to Josie Campobasso; disagreement was out of the question. "So, you and Henry are friends?"

"Something like that." She shrugged, as though she'd never given the topic much thought. "He's nice, but he always has his nose in a book or something. He isn't much for socializing. He's always been that way. Busy." She nodded, satisfied she'd found the very best word to describe Henry. "How do you know him?"

"We're, uh, working on a project together," Miles said carefully.

Josie perked up. "You couldn't have picked a better partner. Henry always wins the science fair. This one year he camouflaged a refrigerator box with branches and leaves, and he spent just about the whole month of April in there, writing down his observations about the nesting behavior of local bird species. It was fascinating. But I'm kind of a bird nut anyway." She pulled a necklace from inside her shirt, showing Miles a small, silver bird charm. "What about you?"

"Sure. Birds are so . . ." He reached for common ground, grasping the first word that popped into his mind. "Feathery."

Josie cocked an eyebrow, like she wasn't sure if Miles was messing with her. "Um, yeah. I guess so. I mostly like them because they fly. Take the ruby-throated hummingbird. Such a tiny little bird, but it migrates from as far south as Panama to as far north as Canada every year." She gazed up in wonder, as if instead of a drop ceiling and fluorescent lights, there was nothing but blue sky overhead. "Can you imagine floating around up there? Warm sun. Cool breeze." She was dreamy-eyed, her voice soothing and hypnotic.

"It's even better than you think," Miles said.

Oops. He'd been so entranced, he'd lowered his defenses. He really needed to work on the whole keeping-secrets thing.

Josie paused for an agonizing moment that seemed to stretch for days. Then she burst out laughing. "For a second, I thought you were going to say you were a bird. I see what you mean, though. We could never understand what it's like to be up there. Airplanes just don't do it justice." Josie scooped up her sandwich for another bite. "So anyway, what class is your project for?"

"It's not for school. It's kind of . . . extracurricular."

"Studying just for the fun if it? No wonder you and Henry get along. Let me know if you need any help. I love seeing the crazy stuff he comes up with."

Miles almost fell out of his seat. Did Josie Campobasso just offer to hang out with him outside of school? Obviously, she could never know what he and Henry were really up to, but that didn't mean they couldn't do something else. But what? What did girls like her do for fun?

It didn't matter. This was Miles's chance, and he was going to seize it. He'd figure out the details later. "Do you think you'd ever want to—"

vrrrrrrr

The phone in Miles's pocket suddenly buzzed to life.

No! Not now! Henry couldn't have picked a worse

time to conduct another one of his stupid tests. Miles was on the verge of a social breakthrough of epic proportions.

vrrrrrrr

"Are you all right?" Josie asked.

"Me? I'm fine. Why?"

"Because you're fidgety all of the sudden."

vrrrrrrr

"It's nothing." Miles searched for Henry in the crowded cafeteria. If he made eye contact with him, maybe he could convince him to back off.

Josie leaned into Miles's line of sight, bringing his attention back to her. "Hello-o. Were you going to ask me something?" Her expression was inviting, telling Miles how she was going to answer his question, if he would only ask it.

Could this really be happening, or was he reading too much into the situation? Only one way to find out.

"I was wondering if . . ." Miles spied something moving in the corner of his eye, and his voice trailed off. He glanced over and was surprised to see Henry across the cafeteria, waving his arms and jumping around like he was trying to get someone to throw him a touchdown pass. Realizing he'd been noticed, Henry stopped jumping and pointed deliberately at his smartphone.

"This is ridiculous," Miles muttered as he reached into his pocket.

"Excuse me?" Josie sounded offended.

"The project I was telling you about. Henry is a little too into it, that's all."

"Right." Josie chuckled bemusedly. "No surprise there. He spent last summer sitting in treetops, so he could draw an aerial map of our neighborhood. He said the images on Google were outdated."

If she continued with the story, Miles didn't hear her. He looked down at his phone, and everything seemed to go still and silent around him. An adrenaline-fueled tremor started in his feet and moved upward as he read Henry's series of texts.

U r on.

Let's go!

NOT A TEST!!!

Miles locked eyes with Henry, who glared admonishingly. He tapped an index finger on his wristwatch—or where his wristwatch would've been, if he wore one. Regardless, there was no mistaking his meaning: Something was wrong, and time was wasting.

"Did you hear anything I said?" Josie asked.

Miles hoped he didn't look as pale as he felt. Why did this have to happen now? "Sure. Listen, we'll talk later, okay?" Miles tossed the remnants of his lunch onto his tray and snatched up his backpack. "I forgot there's something I have to do."

Josie was speechless. She must've thought Miles was joking again. If only he was.

Miles turned and ran, sprinting away from the girl of his dreams.

CHAPTER 14

MILES WAS OUT OF BREATH, HIS HEART STAMPEDING.

"What's the emergency?" he said, panting.

Henry was even. "Have a nice chat?"

"What?"

"No, really. I want to know. Since we have all this time, and nothing of *any* importance *at all* to deal with, we might as well catch up."

"You don't have to be so obnoxious." Miles met Henry's glare with one of his own. "How was I supposed to know you weren't sending me another one of your tests? Ever hear of the boy who cried wolf? You're the kid who texted 'test.'"

"Have you ever heard of the necessity of practice and drilling to meet the requirements for effective emergency response?"

"Actually, no."

"Shocker." Henry's voice dripped with accusation.

Miles was defensive. "Are you going to tell me what's going on or not?"

"Not here." Henry searched the cafeteria for a place where they could talk privately. But in a room filled with more than eight hundred nosy, gossiping students, there weren't that many private places. "Looks like it's the bathroom again," he said, frowning.

They crossed the cafeteria and pushed through the bathroom door. The bathroom was empty, though from the smell of it, it hadn't been that way for very long. Henry leaned against the door to prevent anyone from joining them and bent his head down to study his phone.

"The Gilded Group got a tip about a roadside fire. Probably some jerk tossed a lit cigarette out his window." Most of Georgia had been suffering a drought, and the parched grass and ever-present pine needles on the ground made for good kindling. Despite all of that, some people still viewed the world as their own personal ashtray. "It's spreading quick, and the fire crews can't get their equipment in there to douse it."

Miles exhaled. A brushfire? That was a nice way to ease into things. It wasn't good by any means, but at least it wasn't an alien invasion. "That sounds easy enough," he said.

Henry frowned. "Tell that to the small cavity nesters. Anyway, you're going to want to take I-85 north to Braselton. Just follow the smoke."

Henry was suddenly jolted from behind, nearly causing him to drop his phone.

"Hey!" a voice shouted from the other side of the bathroom door. It sounded like—

"It's Craig!" Henry whispered. "Help me hold the door closed! We can't let him see you change!"

Miles rushed over and pressed his shoulder against the door. The Jammer made a second, more forceful attempt at entry. "Open up!" he growled. "I got one on deck!"

Even with Miles and Henry pushing together, the door started to open. Henry dropped to the floor and tried digging in with his palms and heels, but it was no good. He couldn't find traction on the tile. Gilded would be able to hold the door shut no problem, but there was no way Miles could get the cape on. If he stopped pushing, the door would burst open and throw Henry across the room.

"What do we do?" Miles whispered, panicked. "We can't hold him back forever!"

Henry's face tightened, and Miles imagined a clockwork of gears in his friend's head, all of them turning in search of an answer. Then Henry smiled.

Henry tipped his head back and bellowed an awful moan of discomfort that reverberated off the bathroom walls. "OOOO-WAAAH-OHHH!" It was a cross between a blue whale's call and a lion's roar, if both the whale and the lion were in desperate need of Tums.

Miles plugged his ears. "What're you doing?"

"Scaring him off!" Henry whispered. "Would you go into a bathroom if somebody in there sounded like that?" He grimaced and ground his hands into his gut. "WAAAH-OOO-OHHH!"

"Aw, man!" Craig yelled from the other side of the door. "I hope I didn't eat what you had!" He stopped pushing, and Miles heard footsteps retreating.

Henry ceased his wailing and pressed an ear against the door. All was silent. "It worked! Now get the cape on before somebody else decides to take a bathroom break."

Miles took out the cape, then paused. He stared dumbly at his backpack.

"What are you waiting for?" Henry urged.

Miles held his backpack forward. "What do I do with this? If I leave it here, somebody might swipe it. I already can't afford to replace the books I lost at the construction site. Besides, it has my homework for next period. And if I give my backpack to you, I won't have anywhere to stash the cape when I get back."

Henry folded his hands behind his back, analyzing their predicament. "Try wearing it. Wherever your clothes disappear to when you put on the cape, maybe your backpack will go to the same place."

Miles slid his backpack on. "All right. Here goes." He dropped the cape over his shoulders and touched the clasp halves under his chin.

MAN! THAT NEVER GETS OLD!

ALL RIGHT. OFF TO BRASELTON YOU GO.

MAKE SURE YOU FILL OUT A HALL PASS BEFORE GOING BACK TO CLASS.

HENRY...? HOW AM I SUPPOSED TO GET OUT OF HERE?

NO WINDOWS.

GUESS I COULD PUNCH A *HOLE* THROUGH THE CEILING, BUT THAT WOULDN'T BE VERY *LOW PROFILE...*

I GOT IT! MAYBE I CAN TURN INVISIBLE.

YOU EVER SEEN GILDED BE INVISIBLE IN THE COMICS?

THE *FIRE* IS STILL SPREADING!

WE WON'T *STOP* IT BEFORE IT REACHES *TOWN!*

SHRNN

SHRNN

EVERYTHING'S OKAY! I'M HERE!

STAND BACK.

I'LL BLOW THIS OUT, NO PROBLEM.

WAIT--!

FWOOO

TAKE *THAT*, INFERNO!

YOU... YOU TORE THE WATER TOWER *IN HALF.*

I KNOW!

NO, I MEAN--

I TOTALLY WAS LIKE, *RIIIIP!* HAVE YOU EVER SEEN ANYTHING LIKE THAT? NOT TO BRAG, BUT--

UH-OH. I'M BRAGGING...

GILDED! GILDED! A FEW COMMENTS?

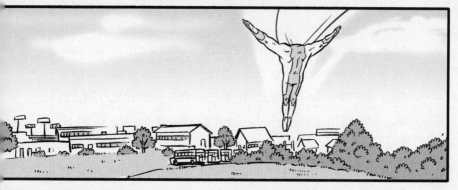

=WHEW=
ALMOST LET
MY EGO GET AWAY
FROM ME BACK
THERE...

WHOOSH

Sure enough, Miles's backpack was on his back, just as it'd been before he put on the cape. So whatever he had on him at the moment he changed into Gilded would still be there when he changed back. Good to know.

Miles stowed the cape and took out the pad of hall passes. He wrote down the time—less than twenty minutes had passed since he flew off to fight the fire—and made up an excuse for his tardiness: "Counseling." That sounded personal enough to not invite prying from Mr. Newton, his fifth-period physical science teacher. Armed with an alibi, he headed off to class.

All eyes were on Miles when he walked through the door. All except Mr. Newton's. He was so wrapped up in his lecture on the laws of motion, he didn't look up from the stack of notes on his lectern.

Miles handed Mr. Newton the hall pass, trying to play it cool, but the paper quivered just enough to betray his nervousness. Not that Mr. Newton noticed. He took the slip from Miles and dropped it onto his desk without so much as giving it a glance.

Miles collapsed into his seat and breathed easy. That hadn't been so bad. Sure, the fire hadn't been put out without a few hiccups, but all things considered, it was a successful mission. The houses were safe. No one had been hurt. Maybe he was putting too much pressure on himself. Maybe looking after the city wouldn't be so tough after all.

vrrrrrrr

Already? Miles's heart jumped into his throat. He'd just gotten himself excused into class. How was he supposed to excuse himself out again?

Thankfully, Henry was only checking in.

Meet me after school.

Henry was waiting for Miles at the bus corral. The remainder of the day had been uneventful, with Henry not even bothering to send any of his test texts. Maybe he'd finally accepted that the phones worked inside the school. That would be a true breakthrough.

Miles strutted over. "So, how about the way I doused that fire? Pretty good, right?" He was intentionally downplaying the event to avoid sounding conceited, but the more he dwelled on his heroics, the more pleased he was with his performance. After all, he'd proven himself to be a one-man fire crew. Not bad for a day's work.

"Mm-hmm," Henry said, his fingers dancing across his smartphone. "I was afraid this might happen." His expression soured, and he slipped the phone back into his bag.

"What's wrong?"

"The town of Braselton doesn't have any water

pressure. People can't take showers or flush their toilets."

"Tell them to call the water department. If that's the big crisis of the moment, then I'd say we're sitting pretty."

"Actually, we're to blame. And by 'we,' I mean 'you.'"

Miles was confused. How was it his problem if someone's indoor plumbing wasn't working? In all those back issues of *Gilded Age*, he seriously doubted there were any adventures where Gilded had to don coveralls and play plumber. "How so?"

"Do you know what the purpose of a water tower is?"

Miles had never really thought about it. "To hold water?" He shrugged.

"Not just hold it," Henry admonished. "Hold it at elevation." He raised one hand to eye level and lowered the other one down by his waist. "A water tower is higher than the buildings it services. Gravity causes the water in the tower to push downward, building up hydrostatic pressure in the system." He lowered his raised hand slowly, pressing down on some invisible force. "When someone opens a faucet, the pressure releases, and the water flows out through the pipes. No water tower, no flow."

Miles leaned against the wall, his shoulders slumped dejectedly. He knew how he'd feel if his apartment suddenly had no running water: not clean. "How mad is everybody?"

"They aren't happy, but they're happier than they'd be if their houses had burned down." Henry waved a hand, brushing the issue away. "Don't worry about it. Once the city gets the pumps up and running, they'll be fine. You, um, might want to help them build a new water tower, though. The old one was a local landmark."

"Of course it was." Miles felt like he'd gone from hero to zero as fast as he could say "flush."

Henry elbowed Miles reassuringly. "It was your first real shift on the job. You saved the day, and you didn't expose your secret identity. Those are the most important things. The rest of this stuff, you'll have to learn as you go. Which means you need to study. A lot." He dropped a hand on Miles's shoulder for emphasis. "Skip the bus. My mom won't be home until five o'clock. Let's get you some more comics to read."

CHAPTER 15

MILES SPENT ALL HIS SPARE TIME BURIED UP TO HIS neck in everything Gilded. When he wasn't reading back issues of *Gilded Age* to bone up on the history of the superhero and what he could do, he was racing from here to there and then over there to protect the city from the people and things that could harm it. In the rare moment of calm when he wasn't doing any of those things, he was busy trying to keep secret the fact that he'd done them. It wasn't easy to not draw attention from neighbors or teachers—or the Jammer, whose quest to torture Miles never let up.

Not drawing attention from his dad was hardest of all. Miles used every trick he could think of. He ate dinner in his room, saying he had too much homework. He pretended to take a shower, leaving the water running and the bathroom door closed. He acted tired—which wasn't really an act—and went to bed early. Any excuse to be alone, so he could slip away at a moment's notice.

Henry was with Miles every step of the way. Sort of. He couldn't accompany Miles on any of his Gilded missions, but he was just as important to the team. He'd used his access to the computers in school administration to swap out PE for shop on Miles's class schedule, so there was no longer any reason Miles couldn't have the cape with him every moment of the day. And Henry was a genius tutor, breaking down class lessons and helping Miles with his homework to keep him from running afoul of his teachers. Or, worse, landing in detention, where he'd be trapped and unable to respond when needed. Henry had a mantra he repeated every chance he got: "Ready for anything."

And Henry meant it. He was relentless with the texting, sending Miles constant updates about breaking news. Henry supplied the time and place of emergencies, and he even devised a rankings system, with the least worrisome events getting a one and the most severe garnering a five. That way, when two or more crises occurred at the same time—something that happened with alarming regularity in a metropolitan area with a population of more than five million—Miles knew which order to tackle them in.

After each crisis was averted, Miles would return home to find more text messages waiting for him. Henry saw each outing as a learning opportunity, and he never failed to point out what Miles had done well and what he could improve on. He had charts on response times and graphs showing the frequency of incidents according to each hour of the day. He assembled opinion polls, using the feedback posted in message boards and from the Gilded Group to gauge Miles's job approval rating. It was as though Miles were running for mayor, and Henry was his one-man campaign staff.

And as good as Henry was at gathering and sifting through information, he was even better at spreading *dis*information. He'd spent enough time as a Gilded fanatic to know that the real threat to their operation wasn't the criminals and catastrophes Miles combatted, but the adoring fans who tracked Gilded's every move. They might mean well, but their desire to know everything about Gilded was the same impulse that could be their hero's undoing. Imagine if one of them actually used the record of Gilded appearances and response times to track Miles back to Cedar Lake Apartments, the way Henry had intended. The next day, there'd be a line of news vans and autograph seekers stretched down Jimmy Carter Boulevard. Not good.

For someone who not long ago was just as fervent as the other die-hard Gilded fans, Henry derived an unsettling amount of glee from throwing them off Miles's trail. He created multiple false online identities for himself and used them to post misleading details about Gilded sightings, even going so far as to say Gilded had gone places where Miles had never gone and been seen doing things Miles had never done. Henry knew from his own efforts to keep tabs on Gilded's whereabouts that a few false data points would be enough to throw anyone's tracking efforts into disarray.

The Gilded Group was the most difficult to dupe, but whenever they started to suspect one of Henry's false identities, Henry used one of his other identities to confirm the made-up reports. Just to keep up appearances, once in a while he'd gang up with the other members and blackball one of his identities, but replacements were only a few keystrokes away. With Henry on the job, Miles knew his identity would stay a secret.

Not that Henry was the only one protecting secrets. Even though Henry wasn't present on any of Miles's outings, eyewitness accounts and news reporters kept him in the loop on what transpired. What happened after, though . . . only Miles knew about that. And he wanted to keep it that way.

For instance, on Thursday he'd saved a runaway freight train from toppling off a broken track. He pressed the two lengths of the fractured track together so tightly, they fused into a single rail. On the way home, Miles had daydreamed about digging for gold, using his bare hands to press his findings into perfect, glittery bars. The cape had shut down in a blink, and he'd crash-landed through the roof of some poor farmer's barn. Add that to his ever-growing to-do list of repairs. At least he'd finally gotten Braselton's water tower back up and running.

Over the weekend, he'd used his supersight to find a five-year-old boy who'd wandered away from his family's campsite and gotten lost in the Oconee National Forest. When he brought the boy back to his family, Miles couldn't help but notice how the boy's fifteen-year-old sister had ogled him. She was no Josie Campobasso, but she was pretty enough to make him consider how easy it'd be to get her phone number. The cape made sure he had plenty of time to ponder the thought, going dormant for two hours and leaving Miles to get lost in the woods himself.

Miles didn't tell Henry about any of that stuff. He couldn't stand to hear another one of Henry's lectures on the true meaning of heroism and that a hero uses his powers only to help others and to do what's right, blah, blah, blah. Easy for him to say. Henry lived in a mansion. He didn't have the threat of the Jammer lurking around every corner. He didn't seem to have any problems at all, really.

More than anything, Miles learned that the hardest part about being a superhero were the cravings. It wasn't the crooks or the crises or the time crunches. It wasn't even that he was on call twenty-four hours a day, seven days a week, though he wouldn't have minded a day off now and then. Resisting the urge to use the cape for things that any normal seventh grader would want to use it for—that was the toughest bit.

Miles didn't have to actually try to misuse the cape, either—all he had to do was think about it, and the cape would go AWOL. What was that about? He was a kid, for crying out loud. He was supposed to look for short-cuts. It was his job to want everything his way.

Miles wished he could talk to the old man and ask him how he'd managed to do it for so many years. All those decades since Gilded first appeared, and there wasn't a single photograph of the old man caught with the cape around his neck, not one reel of news footage showing him crashing into a barn.

The only thing Miles could figure was that it had to do with age. Grown-ups didn't have dreams and desires. They went to work, watched cable news, and were in bed by nine-thirty. If that was all you wanted out of life, you wouldn't be tempted to misuse the cape. Miles's problem was that he was still young and full of imagina-tion.

Yeah, that must be it. More grown-up seriousness, less youthful dreaming. That was the key. If Miles couldn't handle that, then he might as well give up now and turn the cape over to someone more qualified.

But how? How was he supposed to stop himself from thinking?

CHAPTER
16

ONE AFTERNOON, HENRY DISPATCHED MILES TO CATCH
a stray black bear that had wandered into a neighborhood subdivision. It was trash day, and with the home-
owners' cans at the curb, the bear had stumbled upon
a suburban smorgasbord. An eighty-year-old woman
had gone to check her mail and nearly jumped out of
her housecoat when she discovered the bear lunch-
ing on her garbage bin. She called 911, which tipped
off a Gilded fanatic who worked at the police dispatch.
The fanatic posted the incident to the Gilded Group,
and Henry sent Miles a text with the location of the
subdivision and a photo of a black bear, as if Miles
wouldn't know what to look for.

From the moment the elderly woman spotted the
bear, it was only eight minutes until Miles was on
the scene. Not a moment too soon, either, since the
woman's husband had come outside in his bathrobe
and was taking aim at the bear with his duck gun.

That would've definitely ended badly for someone. Probably not the bear.

Miles had swooped down and snatched up the animal, carrying it off to the foothills of the Appalachian Mountains, where Henry said it'd be free to roam. The bear had squirmed at first, but after realizing it was really, really airborne, it threw its paws around Miles and hung on for dear life. Not for the first time, Miles was relieved the Gilded cape was impervious to dirt. He hoped that protection extended to flea and tick bites, too.

Miles returned home and flew through the bedroom window he'd left open, looking forward to a shower. He'd barely had time to take off the cape and hide it in his backpack when he heard his dad's key slide into the dead bolt on the front door.

Miles was thankful he'd beaten him home. His dad had grown increasingly inquisitive about Miles's whereabouts of late, a sure sign he was beginning to detect something strange going on with his son.

"Son? You home?" Mr. Taylor called from the living room. A couple of weeks ago, the question wouldn't have been asked, since there was nowhere else Miles would've been. But then Miles had gone from being a loner to having a seemingly packed social calendar, a meteoric rise for a kid who hadn't known a single soul on the first day of school.

"I'm in my room!" Miles answered. With the cape safely stowed, he flopped onto his bed and grabbed a back issue of *Gilded Age* from the stack on his bedside table. He turned to a random page and started reading just as his dad opened the bedroom door.

Miles glanced over the top of the comic casually. "Hey, Dad."

Mr. Taylor stood in the doorway, holding a bulging manila envelope on one hip. He looked around the room, searching for anything fishy.

"Not studying at Henry's today?" The way Mr. Taylor said Henry's name, it sounded like it should have quotation marks around it, as though he was questioning the existence of the kid his son talked about often but he had yet to meet in person.

Miles's eyes returned to the comic book. "Easy day today. Not much homework."

"No detention, either. You've got a pretty nice streak going, thank the Lord." Mr. Taylor sat on the edge of the bed. "Reading those comics again? Let's have a look."

Before Miles could protest, his dad reached out and plucked the comic book from his hands. Miles sat up quickly. "Be careful with that. It's Henry's. I'm only borrowing it."

Mr. Taylor studied the cover, an artist's rendering of Gilded standing atop a tall, round skyscraper, his gleaming cape billowing in the wind. "Really? This issue has to be thirty years old, if it's a day. I must've read it a million times when I was a kid. Where'd he find it?"

"I don't know. He collects them." Then Miles did a double take. "Wait. You read *Gilded Age*?"

"We all did." Mr. Taylor's expression lit up. "This is the issue where he stops the crime wave that hit downtown in the eighties. Look here." He flipped to a full-page image of Gilded setting down a paddy wagon stuffed with criminals in front of the county jail. "'More guests for the gray-bar hotel!'" Mr. Taylor said, reading Gilded's word balloon aloud.

He closed the comic and gazed at the cover in wonder, looking like a kid himself. "See that round building he's standing on? That's Peachtree Plaza. Back then, it was the tallest building in the city. There's a swanky restaurant at the top that turns in a circle, so you can take in all of Atlanta while you eat. At least I hear there is. I've never been."

"Do you still have your old comics?" Miles asked hopefully. Borrowing from Henry was okay, but it'd be better if he had his own library. For one thing, the pages wouldn't have jelly stains on them.

Mr. Taylor handed the comic book back to Miles. "I wish. You'd have enough reading to last you a lifetime. Your mom tossed them years ago, though."

Miles frowned. "That's all right. Henry has plenty."

"I bet. You should bring him around for dinner sometime. I'd like to meet him. He and me can see who knows more about the Golden Great."

"Sure, I'll ask him," Miles answered, though he had no intention of doing any such thing. Maybe if they still lived at the old house, but Cedar Lake Apartments wasn't the kind of place you showed off to people. Especially not people you wanted to stay friends with.

"Anyway, I've noticed your sudden interest in Gilded, so I got you a little something." Mr. Taylor handed Miles the envelope.

The envelope was lumpy in the middle, but whatever was inside didn't weigh much. The return address said it'd been mailed from Little Rock, Arkansas. As far as Miles was aware, they didn't know anyone in Arkansas.

"Go on. Open it," Mr. Taylor urged.

Miles tore open the top and pulled out a wad of tissue paper wrapped around something hard. He unwrapped the paper, and what he found inside he wouldn't have expected in a million years. In his hand, he held a nine-inch, handmade Gilded action figure.

"Well?" Mr. Taylor asked.

Miles wasn't sure how to answer. If his dad had meant to surprise him, he'd definitely succeeded. "Thanks?"

"No," Mr. Taylor said, grabbing the toy excitedly. "How do you like it? I searched around, and this one was the best I could find. It wasn't cheap, but what the heck. Might as well splurge a little." Mr. Taylor rubbed the toy gingerly, gazing at it with a euphoric grin.

"It's, um, great," Miles lied. Whoever made the toy had obviously spent time on it, but some of the details were wrong. The color of the clasp was off, and the cloth cape had stitching around its border. Henry wouldn't have approved.

"I know!" Mr. Taylor beamed, not detecting the hesitation in Miles's response. "I would've killed for something like this when I was a kid. The best I got was a Gilded throw pillow your great-grandmother crocheted from some leftover yellow yarn."

Realizing he'd been hogging the toy to himself, Mr. Taylor sheepishly handed it back to Miles. "I got this one online. Much better quality. Check it out."

Miles turned the toy over in his hands. If it had been given to him weeks ago, he probably would've liked it. Sure, it was a little lame for a twelve-year-old, but it was still kind of neat—a tiny Gilded he could fit in his pocket.

Miles wasn't the same kid he was weeks ago, though. Had the toy been made since he'd been given the cape? Did the toy maker stare for hours at grainy photos and newsreels of Miles as Gilded, straining to duplicate every detail (but still getting the eyes just a touch off center)? If so, then in a way Miles was holding a miniature version of himself. Identities crashed together in his brain like a five-car pileup. He felt like he was himself and outside himself at the same time. If he pricked the toy with a pin, would he bleed?

Mr. Taylor dropped an arm across Miles's shoulders. It was a rare moment of contact for a man used to staying at arm's length, and it signaled that the conversation was about to get much more serious. "I know why you've been reading those comic books, son."

The blood drained from Miles's face. His insides were a blender churning guilt, fear, and a million other sickening emotions into a thick anxiety puree.

How had Miles ever convinced himself that he'd be able to keep the deception going? Should he have told his dad from the start, no matter what the old man in the garage had warned? He wanted to explain, but he didn't know where to begin. Two words were all he could manage. "I'm sorry."

"Nonsense. There's nothing to apologize for. You had that run-in with the . . . thingamajig from outer space, and it scared you."

"Huh?"

"You're not alone. Everyone is scared. I suspect sales of *Gilded Age* are through the roof right now. It's good to remind yourself once in a while that the whole world isn't your responsibility. That there's someone else out there who'll take care of things. Don't ever forget that."

Miles should've been relieved—his secret hadn't been discovered—but he just felt worse. He'd never thought of things on such a grand scale. The whole *world* was his responsibility. He and Henry had been concentrating just on Atlanta, but there were crimes and catastrophes everywhere, right? How could he ever possibly deal with it all? The invisible weight of it pushed him downward, suffocating him. "I'll try, Dad," he croaked.

Silence fell over the room. Neither Miles nor Mr. Taylor knew what to say, so they said nothing.

vrrrrrrr

The familiar sound was just barely audible coming from inside Miles's backpack.

Uh-oh.

Miles had heard it, no question, but his were young ears. Surely the sound was too muffled to be detected by his dad, whose eardrums had spent more than their share of nine-to-five shifts bombarded by the din of nail guns and jackhammers.

Miles ignored it. Whatever Henry needed, it could wait. Actually, it was entirely possible that whatever Henry needed couldn't wait, but it'd have to wait anyway. Miles already had an emergency on his hands.

vrrrrrrr

"What's that?" Mr. Taylor raised an ear, already homing in on the source of the sound.

"What's what?" Miles answered innocently.

"Don't give me that. I know you hear it. It's sounds like a . . ." His eyes settled on the backpack, then narrowed owlishly. He'd heard the rustle of his quarry and was about to swoop. "What do you have in there, son?"

Mr. Taylor had Miles caught between a rock and a really big rock, and Miles knew it. He could either hand the cell phone over to his dad, or he could let his dad find it himself and discover the cape, too.

Miles trudged over to the backpack and unzipped the pouch with dread. He held the phone forward, offering it in an open palm.

The phone vibrated again, as if to introduce itself.

vrrrrrrr

Mr. Taylor snatched the phone from Miles's hand. "Where'd you get the money to buy this?" he demanded.

"I didn't. Henry gave it to me."

"Henry gave it to you? You're such good pals he's handing out cell phones? You expect me to believe that?" Mr. Taylor was exasperated. "I suppose he's footing your monthly bill, too, since I know you don't have the money to pay it yourself."

"It's prepaid, so there isn't a bill."

"Well, isn't that nice," Mr. Taylor said in a tone that indicated it wasn't nice at all. "I know the times have changed, but I doubt they've changed so much that seventh graders have started paying for each other's phone plans. Henry is some kind of Scrooge, is that it? He's discovered the spirit of Christmas, and he's decided to give all his money away?"

"Actually, it's his parents' money. His dad is an engineer." As soon as Miles said it, he wanted to take it back. He didn't have to continue the thought for his dad to understand exactly what he meant: Henry's dad earned a lot more than an electrician did.

"I see." Mr. Taylor tossed the cell phone onto the bed. "Well, you can tell the engineer's son that the Taylors can take care of themselves. You're going to give that back." He pointed at the phone like it was a juice spill, and he was tasking Miles with cleaning it up.

"But, Dad!" Miles shrieked. "I have to be reachable!"

"Reachable?" Mr. Taylor replied.

Miles had gone from simply being surreptitious to running headlong into disobedience. Disobedience wasn't allowed.

"What's going on with you? I never see you. You

stroll in whenever you want, and when you're home, you're holed up in your room. You've been through some upheaval and I've tried to give you space, but this has gone on long enough. I want answers."

"Henry—"

"I don't want to hear about Henry!" Mr. Taylor's voice grew louder. "Henry isn't my son! You are!"

Miles didn't know what to say, so he didn't say anything.

"Miles, I need this right now like I need a hole in the head. I got a call today that I have to head out to Dobbins on Friday and give a statement about what happened in the parking garage."

Miles blinked. "With who?"

"A General Breckenridge. He wants to know every fascinating detail of what I saw from the pitch-black circuit breaker room I was trapped in. I'll have to use sick time to cover the hours I'm gone from work. Which, at the pace the government moves, will most likely be all day." Mr. Taylor ground his palm against his forehead in frustration.

Miles swallowed hard. "You think they'll want to talk to me?" Miles imagined himself seated at a metal table in a concrete room, a single bare bulb shining in his face. He'd seen enough movies to know he didn't have what it took to withstand a military interrogation.

"Knowing my luck? Absolutely. Which means I'll have to take another day to bring you down. So you'll understand why I'm in no mood to debate with my twelve-year-old about his constitutional right to a cell phone.

"Speaking of which," Mr. Taylor said, marching toward the phone, "if you don't want to give me answers, no problem. I'll see for myself why you need to be so 'reachable.'"

There was nothing left for Miles to do but beg. "Dad, please. Don't."

There was a soft knock on the front door. Mr. Taylor looked back toward the hallway with narrowed eyes. "Now what?" He scowled. Miles had inadvertently goaded his dad into an argument, and now Mr. Taylor was ready to take on all comers.

The knock repeated itself more firmly, and Mr. Taylor stomped from the room with the cell phone clenched in his fist. "Stay put," he instructed Miles. "We're not done discussing this."

Miles waited a moment, then followed his dad. He couldn't help it. No one ever came calling unannounced. Whoever it was, they were very soon going to regret it. Mr. Taylor didn't take kindly to having his scoldings interrupted.

Maybe it was divine intervention, Miles hoped. Maybe some benevolent force had sent an unsuspecting salesman to bear the brunt of Mr. Taylor's anger, so he'd forget all about the phone. Hey, a kid can dream.

Miles came around the corner just as his dad threw open the door. "Who's there?" he bellowed. He sounded like a giant who'd been awoken by a hen-stealing thief.

Mrs. Collins stood in the doorway, her eyes wide like Dixie plates. "Is this a bad time?"

"I . . . uh . . ." Mr. Taylor stammered.

Mrs. Collins leaned her head over to smile past Mr. Taylor. "Hi, Miles," she said.

Mr. Taylor cleared his throat. "No. This isn't a bad time at all. Miles and I were just having a little talk. What can I, um, do for you?"

"Well, it's kind of embarrassing, but . . . Mr. Collins is gone. Like, permanently. You might've noticed it's been a lot quieter around here lately?"

"Good!" Mr. Taylor blurted. Then his face grew redder, and he looked down at his shoes. "I mean, it's good that it's been quieter. Not good that your husband left. That's probably bad."

"Oh, heavens no," Mrs. Collins said with a wave of her hand. "It's for the best, really. Should've happened a long time ago. Only thing is . . ."

"Yes?" Mr. Taylor nudged.

"Well, it's kind of silly, but he took the ceiling fan

with him. See, he claims he bought it with one of his paychecks last year, so it's his by right. He didn't work at all last year, but that's beside the point. Anyway, he packed it up with the rest of his things, and now I just have a bunch of wires hanging out of a hole in my ceiling.

"I bought a new fan this afternoon, and I've seen your work truck, so . . . I was wondering if you'd help me hang it. And by help me, I mean you do all the work, and I'll pour the sweet tea. I just filled some new ice cube trays this morning." She flashed a smile as warm as fresh-baked cookies. "I mean, if it isn't too much trouble."

Who says no to fresh-baked cookies? No one, that's who.

"No trouble at all." Mr. Taylor started gathering his tools, his confidence building as he placed them in the pockets of his tool belt. He always seemed more at ease with screwdrivers and wire strippers in his hands.

"Live wires hanging out of your ceiling? That's no small matter," he said importantly. He set the cell phone on the kitchen counter absentmindedly, then scooped up his tool belt and gave Mrs. Collins a smile. "You came to the right place. I'm as good at hanging ceiling fans as you are at making sweet tea."

Was that charm? Miles could swear he detected a hint of charm.

"Perfect!" Mrs. Collins beamed. "Thanks for letting me borrow your dad, Miles."

"Sure thing, Mrs. . . . uh . . . Miss . . ." What was Miles supposed to call her now, anyway?

"Dawn," she said with a wink. "I'm just Dawn now. I don't want anyone ever calling me 'Mrs. Collins' again."

"Okay. Bye, Dawn." It felt weird calling a grown-up by her first name, but Dawn wasn't like most grown-ups. She was friendly.

"I'll be back in a bit, son," Mr. Taylor said, "and we'll finish . . . whatever it was we were doing." Then he pulled the door closed behind him.

Miles heard Dawn on the landing. "You remember my sweet tea, do you?"

"Yes, ma'am!" Mr. Taylor answered.

The door to Dawn's apartment closed, and they were out of Miles's earshot. If he put on the cape and thought extra-hard about how he wanted to help his dad not blow his chance with the really nice lady who lived next door, would the cape let him use Gilded's superhearing to eavesdrop through the wall? Was that the sort of thing the cape would approve of? He should ask Henry.

Henry!

Miles grabbed up the phone and checked the texts. *18-wheeler jackknifed on I-285.*

3 lanes blocked. Dangerous.

Clean it up?

Miles tapped out a hasty answer. *On it.*

Piece of cake. Miles would have the semi moved off the highway and be back before his dad was finished with the fan.

CHAPTER
17

LORD COMMANDER CALAMITY HAD CONQUERED SO many worlds in his illustrious conquering career, even he couldn't remember them all. There were a handful, though, that he listed as his favorites. Cauldronia III, for example, with its boiling volcanoes and its noxious atmosphere, was definitely among them. A truly Unnd-inviting planet, to step on its surface without a protective suit would cause one's skin to melt away in mere seconds. Oh, how he'd enjoyed sending out the servants who displeased him to retrieve a Cauldronian souvenir, wearing nothing but their thorn pajamas.

Then there was the planet Bottomfrost in the Eyce system. Temperatures so low, when he spat mucus globs, they froze midair and struck the ice-hardened ground with a clatter. At first, the Bottomfrostites were overjoyed when they saw the Lord Commander's battle cruiser descending from the sky. That all changed when it started dropping concussion bombs, and the Bottomfrostites realized the ship hadn't traveled all that way just to whisk them off to a world with a milder climate.

An Unnd-friendly thought occurred to the Lord Commander: He should swap the residents of Cauldronia III and Bottomfrost, to give them each a taste of the other extreme. That would be deliciously Unnd-fair. He made a mental note to do just that when he took his next spring holiday. Nothing relaxed him more than the misery of others.

Cauldronia III and Bottomfrost were worlds the Lord Commander understood, and he admired them for their Unnd-hospitable environments. But as he sat hunched forward on his spiked chair and gazed through the window of his battle cruiser's command bridge, he was confronted with an alien world the likes of which he'd never encountered.

The world consisted primarily of bright blue water that looked so pure, he could taste its coolness in his throat. Anchored amid the enormous seas were vast continents covered in lush greenery surely capable of producing the freshest air ever inhaled by an Unnd's outer nostrils. Suspended in the atmosphere over it all were clumps of a fluffy, white substance that appeared so downy, the Lord Commander could almost feel it tickling his cheek.

"Snarlpustule!" the Lord Commander barked.

Snarlpustule snapped to attention. "Sir!"

"What is that?" The Lord Commander pointed a talon-capped finger at the window.

"Earth, Lord Commander. We have nearly arrived at our target."

"I know the name of the planet, you dungwit! I want to know what *that* is. That . . . quality. How would you describe it? It's causing me to have an odd sensation in this general area right here." The Lord Commander clutched his chest at the place where it covered his heart. (Yes, even a being as heartless as the Lord Commander has a heart. The organ is a biological necessity, after all.)

Snarlpustule raised a confused eyebrow. "Have you been eating your mother's minced hoof pie again, Lord Commander? You know how it gives you acid reflux. Your doctor says—"

The Lord Commander leveled a deadly stare at Snarlpustule. It was an unspoken warning that resonated loud and clear: Don't ever—ever—try to get between the Lord Commander and his mother's minced hoof pie.

Snarlpustule withered.

The Lord Commander turned his gaze on the rest of the command bridge, searching for someone who could give him the answer he sought. "Can't any of you tell me what I'm looking at?"

A meek voice spoke up. "P-perhaps I can be of assistance, L-Lord Commander."

The servant from the Lord Commander's horrible great hall stepped hesitantly from behind a large, armored Unnd warrior. Unsure if he should show respect by making eye contact or bowing, his head bobbed up and down like a shore dragon with an overlarge fish caught in its gullet.

"Very well." The Lord Commander waved the servant forward. He hoped the explanation was satisfactory. He didn't want to behead his best servant. Not when he'd left his favorite beheading implement in his mother's dishwasher back home.

"The quality you're r-reacting to is what's referred to in some c-cultures as 'beauty.'"

"Beauty?" The Lord Commander mused. "I don't understand this word. Translate it into Unnd at once!"

"I'm afraid I c-can't, Lord Commander. No such word exists in the v-vile Unnd language."

"Then describe it!"

"Well, b-beauty is . . . nice. It's, er, pleasant. No, it's better than p-pleasant. It's . . . it's . . ." The servant reached for a better answer, looking as though he wished he'd never spoken up. Then his expression brightened. "It's the opposite of Unnd-attractive!" he declared cheerily.

The Lord Commander was stunned. "And the odd sensation in my chest?"

"That would be e-emotion, Lord Commander. Your subconscious l-longs to be close to Earth's b-beauty, and the tightening f-feeling is a physiological reaction to that desire. It's c-called 'heartache.'"

"Heartache?" The Lord Commander massaged his chest tenderly with his claw. "It sounds repugnant. And I don't mean in a good way."

Snarlpustule poked his own chest curiously. "I'm not experiencing anything."

The Lord Commander looked around at his crew and saw dozens of black eyes looking back at him with confusion.

"Neither am I!" the Lord Commander bellowed. "I was merely testing you lot, searching for weakness. I'll accept no weakness when we're hunting *GGARL!*" The Lord Commander thrust his fist into the air and spat a thick, steaming mucus glob onto the deck of the bridge.

"*GGARL!*" the crew shouted in unison, punctuating their cry with mucous globs of their own. The deck would need refinishing, and there would no doubt be several boots that needed resoling, but the Lord Commander didn't care. He was making a statement here.

"Snarlpustule, begin readying the assault brigade! Full weaponry! And alert the ship's cannon teams. After we've slaughtered this *GGARL!*—"

"GGARL!" Another round of waving fists and mucus globs.

"—and claimed its wretched cape, I want Earth blown to pieces. I'll not allow its . . ."

"B-beauty, Lord Commander," the servant offered.

"Beauty! I'll not allow its beauty to taint my universe!"

"Right away, Lord Commander!" Snarlpustule saluted and ran from the bridge, his cry of *"GGARL!"* echoing after him.

The Lord Commander sat back and looked at Earth one final time. The sight of it really did fill him with a most peculiar feeling. Perhaps there was something there worth saving after all.

No. That sort of thinking wasn't Unnd-natural.

There was no question: Earth must die.

CHAPTER
18

MILES WAS EXHAUSTED WHEN HE RETURNED home from cleaning up the jackknifed semi. He fell into bed, listening to his dad and Dawn laugh through the wall. It was good to hear his dad sound happy.

Even though it was almost dinnertime and Miles was hungry, all he could think about was sleep. He hoped for a quiet night and closed his eyes.

The next day was anything but quiet.

Miles should've known he was in for a wild ride when he rolled out of bed that morning. The apartment was colder than it had any right to be, the result of northern Georgia experiencing its annual in-between season—the time of year when one day feels like summer, the next like fall, and you never know when you go to sleep if you're supposed to have the air-conditioning or the heater on.

Then there was the rain. It ran down the windows in sheets, the wind whipping fat raindrops against the apartment building. No thunder or lightning, though, which meant Miles couldn't use potential electrocution as an excuse to not walk down to the bus. At least the bus stop was covered, so Miles had a place to drip dry after he sloshed through the flooded parking lot to get there.

When he stepped off the bus at Chapman, the sky was dark with swollen clouds. Heavy as the rain was, the storm still had more to give. Miles followed the other kids from the bus and dashed under the overhang. He started to shake himself dry.

Henry was waiting for him, huddled against the building. "Some day, right? I think I took on an inch of rain just getting from my mom's car to here."

"Try waiting for the bus." Miles wrung the bottom of his shirt, and water gushed out.

Henry opened the door to the school, and cold air blasted Miles in the face. Somebody had mistakenly concluded that air-conditioning, not heat, was the way to go. Pneumonia city.

"Look on the bright side," Henry chimed. "Studies have shown that crime goes down twenty-three percent when it rains."

"Maybe so, but I don't need a study to tell me that traffic accidents go up."

"Good point," Henry conceded. "Which reminds me: Nice work with the semi last night. Lots of afternoon commuters tweeted that you helped get them home in time for dinner."

"I'm thrilled they had a restful evening," Miles griped.

Henry eyed Miles with concern. "You all right?"

"Yeah, I'm okay. Just beat. If I'm not crisscrossing the city, I'm wondering when you're going to send me somewhere. Add to that something my dad said last night, which made me realize I'm supposed to be looking after the entire globe, not just my area code. If I'd ever traveled farther than the other side of the Georgia-Tennessee line, that probably would've dawned on me from the get-go."

"You're talking to a Gilded expert. It dawned on me. But if you read the earliest issues of *Gilded Age*, you'll see your predecessor stayed close to home in the beginning, too. First, learn to take care of your city. Then comes the world."

Miles combed his fingers through his rain-slicked hair. "This superhero needs a super-vacation."

"I'll do my best to lighten your workload today. I'll only send you out if it's absolutely necessary."

"It's more than that. All this sneaking around behind my dad's back. It's wearing me down. He found the cell phone, by the way."

"What'd he say?"

"He wasn't happy, I'll tell you that. He got distracted by the neighbor before he could think up a punishment, but you'd better start brainstorming another way for us to keep in touch. If I had to guess, my phone isn't long for this world." Miles thought about mentioning that, on top of everything else, he'd soon be getting grilled by the United States Army, too. But why bother? It wasn't as though Henry would be able to do anything about it.

"I'll come up with something," Henry said. "And before I forget, here." He reached into his bag and pulled out a fresh pad of signed hall passes. "I swear I'll try to take it easy on you, but keep this handy. Just in case."

"Ready for anything," Miles said, frowning. He slipped the pad into his back pocket and trudged off to class.

The wind and heavy rain persisted throughout the morning and into the afternoon. When last period rolled around, Miles found himself in the unfamiliar position of hoping Mrs. Euclid's math lecture wouldn't end, so much did he not relish the idea of going home in the downpour. The National Weather Service should rank the severity of storms according to how many extra minutes of prealgebra one would voluntarily endure to avoid venturing out into them. That's a system that surely every man, woman, and child could relate to.

The patter of raindrops became the harsh clatter

of hail, like the sound of Skittles spilling on a countertop. The lights flickered, and Mrs. Euclid gazed up uneasily. A gust of wind bellowed against the building and dragged a loose tree branch along one of the classroom's windows.

"Children! Move away to the other side of the room!" Mrs. Euclid said urgently.

Then the school's sirens began to wail, and Miles knew, one way or another, he was headed outdoors.

vrrrrrrr

Even before he looked, Miles guessed what Henry was texting about.

Tornado.

F-4. BAD.

Cape up. NOW.

Miles had no clue what made a tornado an F-4, but at the very least, he knew it was more dangerous than Fs 1–3. BAD with a capital B-A-D.

"Attention, all students and faculty," Assistant Principal Harangue's voice squelched over the intercom. "A tornado warning has been issued for Gwinnett County. Please proceed in a quick and orderly fashion to the gymnasium. This is not a drill. Repeat, we are under a tornado warning. This is not a drill."

"Line up, class!" Mrs. Euclid ordered. Kids hurriedly gathered what they could of their belongings and rushed toward the door.

Miles snatched up his backpack and looked for an exit, but he was stuck. The class was bottlenecked in front of the door, waiting for Mrs. Euclid to lead them out. Even if he could somehow get the cape on without anyone seeing—which was doubtful—the only way he'd be able to leave the room was if he busted right through the wall. Not exactly the sort of thing that goes unnoticed.

In the distance a power transformer violently hummed its last breath, and the classroom's lights went dead. The power company would be working overtime tonight.

"Quickly, class! Quickly!" Mrs. Euclid urged.

Miles looked out the window, and that's when he saw it. In the distance, a thick, swirling mass of dark clouds reached down from the sky like a pointer finger of doom. It looked slow and lumbering, but Miles knew that was an illusion. The tornado's winds would be fast enough to rip entire buildings off their foundations. And it was headed straight for the school.

Miles hurried to the back of the line, nervous energy building inside him. Every second that passed was another second the tornado was allowed to cut its path across the ground. Was it picking up cars? Houses? He needed to get outside and help people. He needed to do it now. If he could just make it out to the hallway, then things would be . . .

Worse. The hallway was in chaos. Kids scrambled in every direction like blind bats who'd had their sonar disrupted. Teachers and student hall monitors did their best to herd everyone to safety, but the hallway was choked with people moving in such a disorganized hurry, they forced the entire crowd to move slowly. Only Trisha Brevard seemed oblivious to the danger. She bounced around like a pinball, her head down as she thumbed out a text—probably something along the lines of *OMG! Tornado! LOL!*

The twister was imminent. The building groaned, straining to hold on to its roof. There was no chance they'd all make it to the gym in time. Even if they did, who knew if the building was capable of withstanding an F-4 anyway? It wasn't as if the gym had ever been tested in a wind tunnel.

"Miles!"

Miles spotted Henry getting swept past him by the crowd. He tried fighting his way to Miles, but it was no use.

"Tornados are rotating columns of air!" Henry yelled. "North of the equator, they spin counterclockwise! COUNTERCLOCKWISE!" And then Henry was gone, carried away by the current.

Counterclockwise? Miles didn't have time for fun facts. He needed a place to put on the cape. He could go back inside the classroom, but then what? He couldn't just dash down the hallway like he had during lunch-time. There were too many kids for him to avoid, and if he ran into any of them at supersonic speed, they'd splatter against his chest like lovebugs on a windshield. Miles needed to get clear.

He did the only thing he could think to do. He ran in the opposite direction.

Miles jostled his way against the tide of kids flowing toward the gym. For every step he took forward, he was pushed two steps back.

"Coming through!" he yelled desperately, but no one bothered to make way for him. They just scowled, annoyed by the idiot new kid who was going the wrong way. Miles imagined a bus full of retirees getting sucked up by an F-4 tornado during their outing to the public library, and pushed harder against the throng.

Just as Miles began to wonder if every middle schooler in the county had transferred to Chapman for the day's tornado alarm, the crowd started to thin. The last few older kids shuffled by, snapping their gum and making jokes about how frazzled everyone else was. The coolest of the cool, they apparently felt it necessary to act blasé even in the face of impending natural disaster.

At last, Miles spied light at the end of the hallway— a double-door emergency exit on the west side of the school. He made a break for it. He'd duck into the band room just inside the exit, change, and be airborne without anyone noticing. He was home free.

"Stop!" A voice echoed in the emptying hallway. It was loud enough to be heard above the wailing tornado siren.

Reflexively, Miles stopped short. He recognized that voice. *Whatever you do, don't turn around,* he thought. *Don't turn around!*

Miles turned around. There was Josie, running toward him frantically.

"Oh. Hey, Josie. What's up?" How was it possible for him to utter five simple words and yet sound like a complete dork?

"You're going the wrong way! We're all supposed to head to the gym!" Josie tucked her hair behind her ears, revealing tiny bluebird earrings.

Miles nodded. "Right. Well, I, uh . . ." He reached for something—anything—to say. "I didn't know that. Who told you?"

Josie crossed her arms and pursed her lips, an incredibly gorgeous way of showing she was aggravated. "I'm a hall monitor this period. It's my responsibility to know. And to make sure everyone gets where they're supposed to be."

Whoever decided Josie was the right person for that job, Miles had to commend them on their choice. He'd follow her *into* a tornado, let alone away from one.

Josie softened, and she offered Miles a soothing smile. "Come on, new kid. Follow me."

Yep, right into the swirling, debris-filled heart of an F-one-million tornado.

Josie reached out and took Miles's hand in hers, pulling him gently toward the gym.

Miles was in a trance. Josie Campobasso was holding his hand. Granted, it was because she believed he was too stupid to take adequate cover during a tornado, but still. Josie. Was. Holding. His. Hand. Heart working faster than his brain, it sent word to his feet to do what the prettiest girl in three counties asked. They complied.

He walked slowly at first, but as the worry in Josie's voice grew, so did his speed.

"Hurry!" she urged.

He recognized the nervousness in her tone. It was the fear that creeps in during the final moments before you've reached safety. The fear that fate can't be trusted to bring you the rest of the way home.

How many others were just as scared right now, huddled in their basements or bathtubs, listening to the howling storm outside? Parents clutching their children close. Little kids whose worst nightmares, played against the soundtrack of thunderstorms in the night, seemed to be coming true. All of Chapman

Middle, listening to the groan of the gym as it leaned into the wind.

Miles could make their fears go away.

His brain clamped both hands on the steering wheel and wrestled control away from his heart. His feet planted. Josie walked another step, then was pulled to a stop as well. She wheeled on Miles with eyes wide.

"Let's *go*." Her expression was desperate. She clutched his hand tighter.

"I can't."

"What do you mean, you can't?" Josie barked angrily. She pointed down the hallway. "Move it, Taylor."

Miles couldn't help noticing that she remembered his last name. "You go ahead," he said. "I just realized I, um, forgot something. I'll catch up."

Josie's expression fell. "Please," she whispered.

"I . . ." Josie's eyes were cool, sparkling pools Miles wanted to cannonball into and swim in for days. If he didn't leave her now, he knew he never would. "I'll get to the gym. I promise. But there's something I have to do first."

Miles yanked his hand free from Josie's and sprinted in the opposite direction. A twelve-year-old with zits running from the girl of his dreams—for the second time. Clearly, he was a raving lunatic.

Miles spied the Jammer strolling toward him. Dude the Teammate seemed nervous about taking so long to get to the gym, but not so nervous that he was going to abandon his post at the team captain's side.

The Jammer stopped. He grinned cruelly, fists loaded and ready to do their worst. "Tornado coming, Taylor. Why don't you go outside and play in it?"

Miles dashed past the Jammer without giving him so much as a glance. "Will do!"

Miles ducked into the open band room and slammed the door closed behind him. He made sure the doorknob was locked, then scanned the room for anything that even remotely resembled a changing area. If someone walked past the door, he didn't want to get caught holding a glowing cape.

The drum kit would have to do. He crouched behind the kick drum and tossed his backpack to the floor. Separated from Josie, his mind was back on the task at hand.

The tornado siren pounded on his eardrums. Hail, larger and heavier now, ricocheted like stray golf balls off the windows. Wind buffeted the walls and carried thick tree limbs past. All nature was breaking loose outside. He hoped he hadn't wasted too much time.

The cape hummed on his shoulders, as if to say, "What took you so long?" Miles touched the clasp halves together and felt the surge of power only he knew.

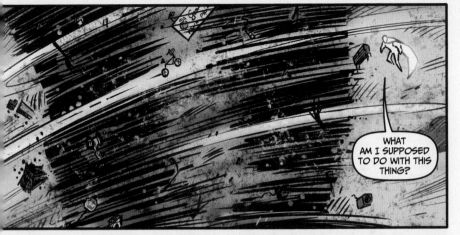

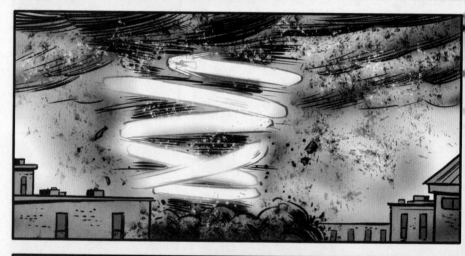

I-IS IT OVER...?

TAKE A LOOK.

YOU DID IT.

YOU DID IT!

DON'T HUG ME!

SORRY.

I'M JUST GLAD THE SCHOOL IS SAFE.

WHAT ABOUT MILES?!

THIS MILES YOU'RE ASKING ABOUT WHO I'VE *NEVER* HEARD OF... YOU'RE, UM, WORRIED ABOUT HIM?

YOU DIDN'T SEE A KID RUN OUT OF THE BUILDING AHEAD OF ME, DID YOU?

"—could you let me come away with a total win?"

At least the cape hadn't blinked out completely. Miles had managed to get control of his thoughts just in time. Still, he had an urge to ball the cape up and toss it into the trees.

True, Miles had saved the school from getting reduced to matchsticks by an F-4 tornado. (A tornado, it was worth mentioning, he had literally flown apart. How cool was that?) But was it really necessary for him to drop his dream girl into a mud puddle just to stop the cape from going dead on him?

To be fair, he'd meant to drop Josie gingerly to the ground, and the mud bath was a result of his lousy aim. Would it have killed the cape to let him cruise around with her for a bit, though? It wasn't like he'd rescued her from death-by-tornado solely to ask her out. How selfish did the cape think he was?

Wait.

Should he ask her out? Would that be cheating? Josie hadn't known she was saying those things to Miles. She'd thought she was talking to a superhero. A grown not-quite-man-but-definitely-adult-something who, for reasons Miles understood all too well, gave new meaning to the phrase "strong, silent type." There was no way Josie believed the things she'd said about Miles would ever find their way to his ears.

Surely there was some kind of rule that prevented

Miles from capitalizing on the information, like the way you can say anything to your doctor or priest and not have to worry about it getting around.

Interesting. That was the word she'd used to describe him. Miles wasn't exactly sure what that meant in girl-speak, but certainly it was better than being uninteresting. She'd said so herself. She liked it.

Let's review: Josie Campobasso had used an adjective to describe Miles, and then she'd said she liked it. Flying a tornado apart was one thing, but this was a miracle. If Miles were forced to use an adjective to describe himself at that moment, it would've been "giddy."

Miles focused, bringing his head back down from the clouds. He'd dealt with the tornado, but a storm that size must have cut a wide swath through the city. There were going to be people who needed medical attention and emergency supplies. Homes and businesses that needed cleaning up.

Miles settled the cape back onto his shoulders and readied himself for another long night.

CHAPTER
19

"SHE ASKED ABOUT ME, HENRY. JOSIE WAS FLYING with a superhero, and she asked about *me*."

"And then you dumped her into a mud puddle," Henry chided. "Not exactly the Pavlovian response you should be aiming for."

Miles blinked.

"As in Ivan Pavlov? The Russian psychologist who pioneered the concept of conditioned reflex? Measured the rate of salivation in dogs coinciding with the ringing of a bell?"

"He studied dog spit? Gross."

"My references are lost on you," Henry replied. "Anyway, consider it a lesson learned. If you try to use the cape to impress girls, you'll only do the opposite. Unless you can find a girl who really likes mud."

It was the day after the tornado. Miles had

snuck out his bedroom window and helped clean up the destruction late into the night. No lives had been lost, but several homes had been carried off in pieces. Thanks to Gilded, the tornado dissipated before too much damage could be done, particularly to Chapman Middle. The school was missing only a handful of roof shingles, plus a single window in the band room, which mysteriously seemed to have been broken out from inside. Tornados were the strangest things.

Now Miles and Henry were in Miles's bedroom. For weeks, Miles had avoided bringing Henry to Cedar Lake Apartments, but Henry wouldn't take no for an answer any longer. Something about the importance of observing Miles in his natural habitat.

Miles still didn't like being in apartment 2H, but over the past months he'd at least become used to it. Seeing Henry standing in the middle of his room threw all the imperfections into sharp relief. The chipped paint. The cracked baseboard. The small water stain on the ceiling from a roof leak waiting to be repaired. Had Henry ever seen a place so meager?

"Happy now?" Miles grumbled. He surreptitiously stepped on an ancient carpet spot, hiding it underfoot.

Henry paced with his hands clasped behind his

back, taking in every detail like a biologist unlocking the secrets of a newly discovered species. He opened the closet and poked his head inside. "Fascinating," he said, nodding.

Miles couldn't imagine what was so fascinating about his dirty socks, but apparently they held great scientific significance.

Henry shut the closet and moved over to the desk. His eyes settled on the handmade Gilded action figure, and he stopped short. "Decent job on the costume," he muttered to himself. He picked up the toy and began turning it over in his hands. "Details are a little sketchy, but that's to be expected. Its presence does suggest a burgeoning narcissism, though. I'll need to keep an eye on that."

Miles snatched the toy from Henry. "Are you just about finished dissecting my private life?" he scowled. "For your information, my dad bought this for me. I'm too old to collect Gilded toys. Unlike *some* people, whose names I won't mention."

If Henry detected the insult aimed at him, he didn't let on. He crossed his arms and nodded at his surroundings approvingly. "Fairly secluded. A window for coming and going undetected. As far as hideouts go, it isn't the Batcave, but it could be a lot worse."

Henry plopped down onto Miles's bed and appraised the tidy stack of *Gilded Age* comics on the nightstand. "Looks like you've been doing your homework." He reached for his shoulder bag. "I brought more reference material for you. You're doing good, but this isn't the time to rest on your laurels. Not until you stop, you know, dropping helpless schoolgirls from the sky."

boom

Henry's ears perked up like a guard dog after hearing the rattle of a chain-link fence. "That's strange. I don't remember seeing a forecast for more storms." He glanced out the window, scanning the sky for gray clouds. "I'd better see if there's another tornado watch in effect."

Boom

Miles's blood turned to ice, the memory of a recent day at a parking garage rushing into his head. "Henry," he breathed. "That isn't a storm."

They locked eyes, and everything that needed to be said was communicated without a word between them.

"TV," Henry said.

They raced to the living room. Miles snatched up the remote control. He turned on the TV, trying to convince himself that what he knew was happening wasn't happening. That the truth was a lie. Maybe it really was just a storm.

BOOOMBLLL!

The windows rattled, and Miles heard the dishes jump in the kitchen cupboard. Nope. Definitely not a storm.

"Too loud," Miles moaned. "If it's happening in the city again, we should barely be able to hear it all the way out here. You think they're closer to where we are?"

"Either that, or this time . . ." An emergency news broadcast filled the TV screen, and Henry caught his breath. "There's more of them."

Miles's heart dropped through his stomach and into the downstairs apartment. "More" was the understatement of the year. The live news feed showed a spaceship—a ginormous, hulking spaceship—engines booming in fiery bursts as it lowered itself over downtown. People stood on the sidewalk or stopped their cars in the street, gazing upward in terror.

"It's difficult to describe what we're looking at," the reporter said. "The aliens have returned, seemingly in full force. But why are they here? What do they want from us?"

The spaceship was the kind of thing Miles had

imagined when he was little, dreaming how cool it'd be if things like it actually existed. Well, guess what? Apparently, they do exist. Miles was staring at one right now, and it was extremely *not* cool. It wasn't bulbous and smooth, like the ships good aliens always use in movies to tool around the universe. It was angled and jagged, like a dagger designed for stabbing entire planets in the gut. It was a bad-alien ship. No doubt about it.

As if to prove him right, massive doors in the ship's side slid open, releasing a swarm of aliens on flying sleds.

"Not again," the reporter whined. Poor guy had probably leaped eagerly from the news van, excited about landing the story of a lifetime. Now he realized that his lifetime was most likely going to be cut extremely short.

The aliens opened fire. A building exploded, raining rubble on the street below. Another blast chewed a hole in the ground, sending massive chunks of asphalt into the air. People screamed and ran, but there was nowhere to run to. The aliens were everywhere.

Miles suddenly had a terrifying thought: Where was his dad? He tried to remember if his dad was back to working at the downtown parking garage.

That project had to be finished by now, didn't it? He desperately hoped so.

"Ready for anything," Henry stated.

Miles didn't know whether to be flabbergasted by Henry's matter-of-factness, or hopeful that it meant he had a plan. He chose the latter. "You know what to do about this, right?"

A man in a business suit ran screaming past the camera. Henry frowned. "Not a chance. I mean, are you watching? We're being colonized by an apex species. I have no earthly idea what to do about it." He looked at Miles gravely. "But this is what I've been training you for, and you're going to find a way to stop them."

"Training?" Miles was confused. "I tipped over a water tower. I lugged a stray bear up to the mountains. How exactly does any of that classify as training?"

"Granted, it'd be better if you had more experience with less . . . typical crises. But all the missions I've sent you on—battling car wrecks and fires and, yes, even stray bears—it wasn't just to see how exhausted I could make you. It was to prove that you're up to the challenge. The challenge of being Gilded."

Miles watched pandemonium unfold on the TV.

He'd never felt so inadequate in his life. "I don't blame you for doubting me."

Henry placed a firm hand on Miles's shoulder. "I wasn't trying to prove it to me. I was trying to prove it to *you*. You needed to believe that you're capable of so much more than you ever imagined."

"But this . . ." Miles trailed off. All at once he understood why the old man had given up the cape. He'd surmised he wasn't strong enough to face a challenge of this magnitude. And if he wasn't, how could Miles possibly be? "I can't, Henry. I'm just not good enough."

Henry smiled encouragingly. "You've given everything to keep this city safe. Now you're going to do it again."

"How can you be sure?"

"Look. If I say I know you'll come home, I'll be lying. But you've got to try. Heroes aren't heroic because they fight when they know they're going to win. They're heroic because they fight even when they know they're going to lose."

The front door burst open. Mr. Taylor stood breathless in the doorway with Dawn a step behind him. "Miles! Thank the Lord, you're home!"

"Dad!" Miles rushed over and hugged him. "I was scared you were downtown." He was scared about so much more, too. Scared in a way that not even holding on to his dad could help.

"I took a long lunch. I had a, uh, hankering for Biscuit Barrel." He glanced at Dawn, who, Miles noticed, was wearing her waitress apron. She looked frazzled, which was understandable considering she couldn't have known when she left for work that morning that her shift would end with an alien invasion. She walked slowly toward the TV, fear written all over her face.

"The cook heard it on his radio," she said. "Oh God. It's really happening."

"Pack your stuff, Miles," Mr. Taylor ordered. He turned to Dawn. "You do the same. The three of us are heading north, toot sweet."

Dawn nodded. "Be right back."

Dawn rushed from the apartment, and Mr. Taylor turned back to Miles. "You're standing, son. Why are aren't you moving?" Then he noticed Henry for the first time. "Who's this watching my TV?"

Henry stuck out his hand. "Pardon my rudeness, sir. Henry Matte. I'm pleased to make your acquaintance."

Mr. Taylor's eyes narrowed. "So you're the infamous Henry, the man with the many cell phones. I wouldn't mind chewing the fat with you, but this hardly seems the time. I'm sure your parents are beside themselves right now."

"I don't doubt it, sir."

Mr. Taylor pressed his lips together in a tight frown. "Tell me where you live. I'll drop you home on our way out of town."

"I'm not going home, sir. And Miles can't leave with you."

"The heck?" Mr. Taylor was getting mad now.

Miles swallowed hard. "He's right, Dad. I have to stay."

Mr. Taylor fumed. "I'm on the verge of being real angry here!" There was nothing on-the-verge about it.

Miles knew what he had to do. There was no longer any choice. He'd worked so hard to keep the secret, but the only way to go on keeping it would be for him to get in his dad's work truck and head away from danger. Leave behind Atlanta and its millions of helpless, terrified citizens. Trade his life for all of theirs. It was tempting—boy, was it ever tempting—but it'd also be wrong.

"Dad, I have to tell you something."

Henry clamped a hand over Miles's arm. "Miles . . . are you sure?"

Miles had to fight. He had to try. But first, he had to convince his dad to let him. "If I don't tell him, he won't let me stay."

"Somebody better tell me something," Mr. Taylor growled. "Fast. Like why I got two twelve-year-olds in front of me, both of them acting like I'm not the only adult in the room."

"Wait here, Dad."

Miles left Henry alone with his dad and hurried to his bedroom. As he yanked back the zipper on his backpack, he could feel the entire bag vibrating. Gold light spilled out of the open pocket, bathing Miles in its glow.

"You and me, cape," Miles breathed. "Try not to get me killed."

Miles rushed back to the living room, where his dad stood with puffed cheeks and flexed hands. He looked like a rocket about to blast off.

"Maybe you'd prefer to sit, sir," Henry offered genially.

"All right." Mr. Taylor lowered himself to the sofa, then leaped back to his feet. "Now, just hold on. Don't tell me what I'd prefer to do in my own living room. I want to see some feet marching toward the front door, or I'm going to start carrying folks."

"It's okay, Dad." Miles held the cape forward. It shone brighter than it ever had before, as though it sensed the army of lizard-monsters close at hand. "Henry is only trying to prepare you for the shock."

Mr. Taylor looked at Miles, and then the cape, and then back at Miles again. "You've got a glow-in-the-dark blankie?" he said, frowning.

Miles stepped closer, showing Mr. Taylor the clasp. "Not a blankie. It's a cape. *The* cape. Gilded's cape."

Mr. Taylor's face tightened, and he spoke through clenched teeth. "What kind of foolishness has gotten into you, boy? It's the end times outside, and you're playing games?"

Miles understood his dad's reaction. It was ridiculous. Utterly and completely preposterous. That didn't change the fact that it was true. "No games. It's the real deal. Swear on Grandma's grave."

Mr. Taylor jolted like a bucket of ice water had been introduced to his face. Miles had invoked the one and only phrase that guaranteed what followed was the 100 percent, God's honest truth. Taylors might tell a tall tale once in a while. Sometimes they might even outright fib. You best believe they didn't do it in the presence of a grandmother's grave, though. Not ever. That Grandma Taylor was still very much alive and probably baking a pie at that very moment was irrelevant. The gravity of using "Grandma" and "grave" in the same sentence spoke for itself.

"Grandma's grave . . . ?" Mr. Taylor reached out

tentatively, allowing his hand to brush against the cape. He pulled it back as if he'd been shocked. "It's . . . humming."

Miles nodded. "It knows when it's needed. Don't ask me how, but it knows."

Mr. Taylor tried to process what he was hearing. "So you're Gilded's, what, sidekick or something? You look after his cape when he's not using it?"

"It's interesting you went there," Henry chimed in. "My first reaction was shape-shifter, but I can see why you'd think—"

"You're not helping," Miles interrupted.

"Right. Sorry."

"Dad, remember the old man in the parking garage? He was Gilded. At least, he was the Gilded you read about in those comics when you were a kid. Before he died that day, he gave me this cape and said I had to be the new Gilded. So that's what I've been doing for the past few weeks. With Henry's help."

"You might say I'm the brains of this world-saving operation," Henry said, beaming.

"That's the reason I have the cell phone. Henry lets me know where and when there's an emergency, which is pretty much all the time. Being a superhero isn't exactly a nine-to-five job." Miles took a deep breath, knowing that once he said the next words, there'd be no turning back. "And that's why I won't leave with you. The city needs me."

"You're telling me the hero who's been flying all over town—the guy fighting robbers and tornadoes—is you?" Mr. Taylor shook his head in disbelief. "That's not possible."

On the TV, a line of military vehicles stormed into downtown, soldiers leaping to the ground. Through the shaky video feed, Miles glimpsed the man with the bottle-brush mustache who'd taken charge at the parking garage. Only now did Miles remember that the news had called him General Breckenridge—the same General Breckenridge who planned to get a statement from Miles's dad about the alien in the garage. Well, if the General wanted to learn about aliens, he was about to get a firsthand lesson. The hard way.

"There's only one way I can think to convince you," Miles said, taking a step back from his dad. "Keep your distance. I'm about to get bigger."

He placed the cape over his shoulders, thinking how he needed to prove he was Gilded, so his dad would let him try to save the world from annihilation. Emphasis on "try."

The last sound Miles heard was a woman's scream coming from the TV. Power poured into him, and the clasp halves leaped from his hands.

NEITHER DO YOU. THERE'S AN *ARMY* ON THE TV. WHAT EXACTLY DO YOU THINK YOU CAN DO?

CONVINCE THEM THEY CAN'T BEAT ME. OR FIGHT THEM UNTIL THEY DO.

I CAN'T BELIEVE I'M TALKING TO MY *TWELVE-YEAR-OLD* ABOUT WHETHER HE SHOULD BE ALLOWED TO RESCUE THE PLANET FROM *SPACE GATORS.*

GIVE ME THE CAPE. I'LL GO.

IT DOESN'T WORK LIKE THAT.

HOW HARD CAN IT BE? YOU JUST PUT IT ON AND

WHOOP!

THERE'S MORE TO IT. *A LOT* MORE.

LISTEN TO HIM, MR. TAYLOR.

THE CAPE TAKES DISCIPLINE AND TRAINING TO USE IT.

AND AS ABSOLUTELY, ONE-HUNDRED-PERCENT *INSANE* AS IT SOUNDS, MILES IS THE MOST DISCIPLINED AND TRAINED CHANCE WE HAVE.

IT HAS TO BE HIM.

GEE, *THANKS.*

DON'T MENTION IT.

DEAR GOD IN HEAVEN...

I'M JUST AS SCARED AS YOU. BUT THE FACT THE CAPE IS STILL WORKING IS *PROOF* THAT ME GOING IS THE RIGHT THING TO DO.

TRUST ME?

CHAPTER
20

IMAGINE LYING OUT AT THE LAKE UNTIL YOU HAVE A blistering sunburn, then ironing your dress shirt—while you're wearing it. That's what it felt like to get shot by an Unnd weapon.

The cape's power fled from Miles, and in its place was nothing but searing agony. Waves of it pulsed over him from head to toe and back again. When the giant alien with the doubled-bladed doohickey had blasted him, it felt like nothing in the world. Which made sense because it wasn't.

He rubbed a hand across his burning chest, and all he could think of was home. Not Cedar Lake Apartments, but some other home he and his father could start far away from Atlanta and the swarm of aliens who wanted to wipe the city off the map. If only the cape would take him away. He'd grab his dad and go someplace safe. Henry could join them, if he wanted.

Just one last flight, and he'd never wear the cape again. He promised.

The cape wasn't responding, though. Miles's impulse to run away was most certainly the reason it'd stopped working in the first place. Fleeing to save yourself was a thought entertained by cowards. It was everything the cape could never be. Hadn't the old man fought to his last dying breath?

"GYARRGH!" the giant alien who'd blasted him bellowed. The cry reverberated down the street. Windows shattered.

Through the gaping hole created when Miles crashed into the building, he watched the alien lift the front bumper of Mr. Taylor's truck with one hand. The alien sneered and spat in a guttural language Miles could no longer understand, but its meaning was obvious—it was going to toss the vehicle bought and paid for by Atlanta Voltco like a Frisbee.

"Look alive!" Mr. Taylor yelled.

He and Henry tumbled from the truck's open doors just as the alien launched it into the third floor of an office tower. It landed with a crunch, its rear end hanging out of the building.

Miles had never felt so hopeless as he did at that moment. His dad had plowed into the alien at full speed, crumpling the front of the truck on impact. Still, the alien showed no sign of injury.

It strode over to Mr. Taylor and Henry, who sat huddled together in the street. It garbled something that Miles could only guess was a threat of the no-ears-or-head-to-hang-them-on variety.

Henry turned to Mr. Taylor and saluted stoically. "Mr. Taylor, it's been an honor serving with you."

Mr. Taylor blinked. "You are, beyond a doubt, the strangest kid I've ever met."

The giant alien lowered the tip of its weapon, aiming it at Mr. Taylor and Henry.

Henry gulped as Mr. Taylor scanned the street, finding Miles amid the rubble the way only a father searching for his son could. Blue eyes met blues eyes. Taylor eyes.

"You can do it, son."

Time slowed to an uphill crawl.

Miles watched General Breckenridge and his soldiers fight with everything they had against an army from beyond the stars.

He saw his dad, who worked so hard to give Miles the best life he could. Who'd charged into battle against the aliens armed with only a pickup truck.

There was Henry, the smallest seventh grader at Chapman, who'd dedicated himself to helping Miles without ever once asking what was in it for him.

And Miles thought of Josie. Beauty wasn't the only thing that drew him to her (though it certainly didn't hurt). He liked her because she was the type of girl who sat where she wanted at lunch, regardless of what others might say. She was the type of girl who braved an F-4 tornado to try to save a kid she hardly knew.

A realization hit Miles like a lightning bolt out of the blue: Everyone had the ability to be a hero.

The tip of the giant alien's weapon glowed red. Some beast with acid snot was planting its claws in Miles's hometown, pointing a death-ray hockey stick at the people he cared about.

What was he going to do about it?

He was going to fight, that's what. Maybe he didn't have a chance against all those lizard-monsters, but his dad always said anything worth doing wasn't easy. So he'd keep fighting until either he or the lizard-monsters didn't have any fight left to give.

Not because he wasn't scared. Not because he wanted to. He was going to do it because it was the right thing to do. And he was the only one in the world who could do it.

The clasp halves rose from his chest on their own, eager to get back in the battle. Miles's pain evaporated, replaced with more power and energy than he'd ever experienced before. He was a thoroughbred racehorse straining at the gate. A rocket on the launch pad, engines rumbling.

Do the clothes make the man, or is it the other way around?

Only one way to find out.

THEY'RE ON THE RUN! *CHASE* THEM!

WE CANNOT. THEY HAVE GIVEN UP THE FIGHT. TO STILL ATTACK THEM WOULD BE...RUDE.

YOU WEAR THE GOLDEN CAPE WELL, STRANGER. AXILOM WOULD BE PROUD.

AXILOM...?

ONE OF OUR *GREATEST* CHAMPIONS... AND MY BEST FRIEND.

WE LOST CONTACT WITH HIM SOME TIME AGO. HIS SHIP MUST HAVE CRASHED SOMEWHERE ON YOUR WORLD...

WHEN ONE OF OUR SCOUTS DETECTED CALAMITY'S INVASION FORCE APPROACHING THIS SOLAR SYSTEM, WE FEARED THEY HAD LOCATED AXILOM.

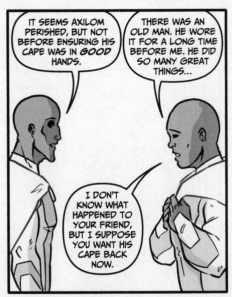

IT SEEMS AXILOM PERISHED, BUT NOT BEFORE ENSURING HIS CAPE WAS IN *GOOD* HANDS.

THERE WAS AN OLD MAN. HE WORE IT FOR A LONG TIME BEFORE ME. HE DID SO MANY GREAT THINGS...

I DON'T KNOW WHAT HAPPENED TO YOUR FRIEND, BUT I SUPPOSE YOU WANT HIS CAPE BACK NOW.

NO. YOU HAVE PROVED YOURSELF WORTHY.

IT IS YOURS BY RIGHT.

BESIDES, THE UNIVERSE WILL BE MORE AWARE OF EARTH NOW. AS YOU HAVE SEEN TODAY, THAT WILL NOT ALWAYS BE A *POSITIVE* THING.

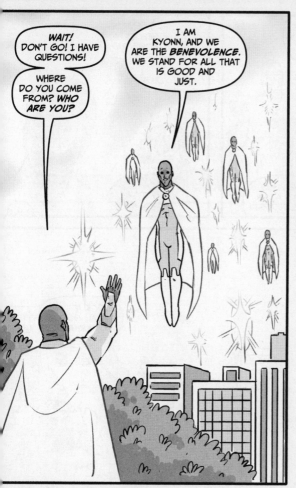

CHAPTER
21

WHAT DID THE PRESS DO WHEN THEY COULDN'T
interview the Golden Great, the Halcyon Hero, the
Twenty-Four-Karat Champion who thwarted plan-
etary decimation? They interviewed everyone else.

Meter maids. Window washers. Citizens walking their dogs. Parking a space cruiser over a major
metropolitan area lends itself to a herd of eyewit-
nesses. There was no one the press talked to more,
however, than Hollis Taylor, the valiant electrician
who charged into the fray with his fully loaded Ford.

Miles's dad had Dawn come pick him and Henry
up from the attack zone, and they hoped that'd be
the end of it. Turns out, though, that leaving your
work truck parked in the third-story window of
an office building makes you a fairly easy person
to track down. With the military cordoning off
downtown again, Mr. Taylor soon became the best
story in the city. Or, at least, the most accessible.

There were phone calls around the clock. Reporters followed him to and from work. Faces Miles had only ever seen on TV dropped by unannounced and invited themselves in, snapping photos and filming impromptu tours of apartment 2H. Mr. Taylor stopped by Krispy Kreme for coffee one morning, and they gave it to him on the house. In other words, he was famous.

By extension, so was Miles. The kid with the stack of *Gilded Age* comic books wound up with a real-life hero for a father. The feel-good headlines wrote themselves. Miles was sure that Henry would blow a gasket over all the attention, but he loved every minute of it. He called it "hiding in plain sight."

All the while, Miles's backpack went undisturbed. Not once did a reporter ever think to ask what was inside.

By the third night following the foiled invasion, Mr. Taylor was a household name. After a busy evening of interviews, he was ushering out the last reporter, an anchorwoman from a national morning show who'd just finished the grand tour, stack of comics and all. Just as he closed the door behind her, the kitchen phone rang.

"Lord, do I ever need an answering machine for this nonsense," he muttered as he lifted the phone from the cradle. "Interview time is over," he barked. "Call back tomorrow." A moment paused, and he sighed heavily. "Hi."

Miles knew that "Hi." It was the "Hi" that meant his mom was on the line. She'd called every night since the "event," as she referred to it. She couldn't seem to wrap her head around the fact that a murderous alien mob had rampaged in her old hometown.

"No, Eve. I didn't—

"That's not what—

"It's not like I asked to be—

"Aw, what's the use?" Unable to get a word in, Mr. Taylor held out the phone to Miles. "Talk to your mother, son."

Miles reached for the phone, but his dad suddenly pulled it back. He gave Miles the look he'd given him after the time they went off-roading with Uncle Cole and nearly flipped the four-wheeler. It was a look that said, *Talk to her, but don't tell her too much.*

Miles nodded and took the phone. "Hey, Mom. How are you?"

"How am I? I'm worried out of my mind, after all that's happened. How are you?"

"I'm okay, Mom," Miles said. "Honest. I know it sounds weird, but I'm really not that freaked out."

"You swear on Grandma's grave?"

"I swear on Grandma's grave."

Mr. Taylor gave Miles a thumb's-up.

Miles's mom was quiet for a moment, and when she spoke again, her voice was heavier. "I'm sorry, Miles. I'm just concerned. Why does this keep happening in Atlanta? Can't the Martians burn down a cornfield or something for a change?"

Miles knew why the Unnd had attacked Atlanta. They wanted Gilded's cape. If he told his mom that, explained how he knew, would she come home? Maybe, but that would be using the cape for selfish reasons, and no good would come from it. Not for Miles, and certainly not for his parents. Facts were facts. They just weren't right for each other.

"I think it's lucky they came to Atlanta," Miles said. "That's where Gilded is, so he was able to stop them. If they were smart, they would've gone anywhere else."

"You sound just like your father." His mom sighed. "When we were younger, he used to go on and on about Gilded. Absolutely adored him. I suppose that's what put that harebrained notion in his head to play chicken with one of those things. He always wanted to be a hero. But you can't be a dreamer all your life, Miles. Someday, everyone has to grow up."

Miles glanced at his dad, who looked nervous enough to gnaw his fingers down to their second knuckles. "He did good, Mom. He did really good."

vrrrrrrr

Miles reached for his cell phone and checked the screen. It was nice to be able to do that without having to hide from his dad.

Peachtree Plaza damaged.

Structure needs shoring up.

Things had been quiet since the attack—most of Miles's calls dealt with assisting the cleanup and repair crews. Apparently, wide-scale alien invasions make even criminals want to hunker down indoors. Still, the job needed tending to.

"I have to go, Mom. Things are still a little bonkers here."

"Be safe, okay? I meant what I said. Maybe Jack and I can have you down here during the winter break."

"That sounds good." A trip to Florida couldn't be all bad, could it? Besides, whether Miles wanted to admit it or not, he missed her.

"I love you, Miles."

Miles knew she meant it. It was just that, after twelve years of motherhood, he wished she knew how to show it a little better.

"Love you, too, Mom."

Miles set the phone back in its cradle and tapped out a response to Henry.

"Headed somewhere?" Mr. Taylor asked.

"Peachtree Plaza," Miles replied. "I shouldn't be gone long."

Mr. Taylor combed a hand through his hair and let out a long breath. "I guess we ought to talk about all this, huh? You being a superhero on a school night and everything."

Miles knew this conversation would need to happen, but he dreaded that it was finally here. "Do we have to do it now?"

Mr. Taylor pulled Miles close and gave him a strong hug. "Just don't sleep through your alarm. If I have to drive you to school, it'll cut into my hours, and my paycheck needs all the help it can get."

Miles was stunned. "Is that it?"

Mr. Taylor smiled. "I can't exactly tell you to quit protecting the free world, can I? Now go on, son. Make me proud."

"You almost got me killed, you know."

Miles shut his locker and turned to find Josie scowling at him. School had been closed for the past three days on account of the Unnd attack, so today was the first time the students had been under the same roof since the tornado. Saying that he and

Josie had a lot to talk about was an understatement.

"Right. About that . . ." Miles searched for an excuse and blurted the first one that popped into his head. "I was really scared."

No sooner than he said the words, he wanted to cram them back into his mouth with his fist. *Make yourself sound like a chicken. Good thinking. That's sure to win her over.*

He did his best to change the subject. "At least you met Gilded. That must've been cool."

Miles wasn't revealing anything he wasn't supposed to know. Word about Josie taking a flight with Gilded began to spread the minute she'd splashed down. Josie had always been popular. Now she was all the rage.

"Oh, that," Josie said. "I know. Pretty crazy."

"What's he like?" Miles pressed.

Josie considered the question for a moment, then shrugged. "He's a superhero who can fly and blow apart tornados. He isn't like anything."

"Right. Sorry. Dumb question." Miles's inability to make casual conversation was on full display, as usual.

Josie cracked a smile. "Anyway, I just wanted to make a request. If we're ever in the same place when a tornado touches down, do me a favor and run *away* from it."

Miles smiled back. "Away from tornados. Gotcha."

A long silence passed. Josie drummed her fingers against the textbook held to her chest. Her smile faded.

"Um . . . guess I'll go to class then. Bye." She turned and headed down the hallway.

Miles watched her go, a hummingbird on the wing. He wanted to say something, but his tongue felt twelve sizes too big. What chance could he ever have with a girl like her? Better to let her flutter away.

Then again, why couldn't he have a chance with Josie?

Maybe Miles didn't have a lot of friends. He definitely wasn't a heartthrob or a star athlete or any of the other things that girls always went for. But he'd stopped armed kidnappers, natural disasters, and the hugest threat planet Earth had ever seen. Not because he was popular or good-looking or could throw a tight spiral. The cape didn't care about that stuff.

The cape had allowed Miles to do all those things because it had judged him to be a hero. He was *good*—deep down inside, where it mattered. That counted for something, right?

"Josie! Wait!"

Josie turned back, her hair falling across her shoulder just so. "What?"

Miles got lost in her hazel eyes, his moment of courage slipping away. And he thought fighting lizard-monsters was tough.

"I was wondering if . . . I mean, do you like to? Maybe we could—"

"Quit it!" a voice yelled. It was a desperate cry that brought the rest of the hallway to dead silence.

He and Josie looked and saw a small, thin kid—Miles recognized him, but didn't know his name—scrambling to take back his sack lunch from Craig. Craig didn't have to do much more than hold it up to keep it out of the kid's reach.

"Please?" the kid pleaded softly.

"Please what? It says 'rob,' so I'm robbing it." Craig kept the brown bag aloft but rotated it enough to show the letters R-O-B written in a woman's cursive script.

The kid's mom still wrote his name on his lunch? Parents never understand how easy it is to ruin their child's life.

Craig tossed the bag to Dude the Teammate, who rummaged through the contents and pulled out some Nutter Butters. "Dude!" he exclaimed cheerily, biting into one of the peanut-shaped cookies.

Miles was infuriated. He strode toward Craig with fists clenched.

"Congratulations, Craig. You read three whole letters all by yourself. I'm glad the tutoring is finally paying off."

"Three?" Henry stepped forward to stand beside Miles. He must've been lurking nearby, giving Miles and Josie their space. "Last I heard, the tutor had only taught him two letters. Craig here cracked that third one all by himself."

"Attaboy, Jammer," Miles jeered. "High five." Miles raised his palm in the air, stopping it in front of Craig's face.

The Jammer flinched.

"Dude?" Dude the Teammate was stunned. Miles Taylor had made the Jammer flinch.

Somewhere in the crowd, a kid snickered. Craig narrowed his eyes, searching for the offender. Then he turned his attention back to Miles.

"You never learn, do you, Taylor?" he growled.

"No, I guess I don't." Miles guessed he didn't.

"See if this sinks in."

Craig palmed Miles's face like a football and shoved him backward. Miles lost his footing and plopped to his butt on the cold terrazzo floor. The crowd burst into laughter.

"Later, Taylor." Craig snatched the sack lunch from Dude the Teammate and slam-dunked it into the trash. The recycling bin, not the bin for general waste. The Jammer's evil was truly diabolical.

The crowd thinned out, until it was just Miles, Henry, Josie, and poor Rob. Miles picked himself up and retrieved the sack lunch from the garbage. He dusted it off and handed it to Rob with an encouraging smile. "Good as new. Don't let the idiots get to you."

"Thanks for the help," Rob said. He risked a glance at Josie, blushed, and then headed off to class.

"Speaking of idiots," Henry said. "What were you thinking, Miles?"

Miles looked down and smoothed his shirt. "I wasn't. Obviously."

"Very obviously." Josie put her hands on the straps of Miles's backpack and adjusted it for him. "It was a nice thing you did, though. Brave, too. I see where your dad gets it from."

"My dad?"

"Sure. He's the one who rammed that alien with his work truck, right?"

Miles blinked. "You know about that?"

"Miles, *everyone* knows about that. Nice stack of *Gilded Age* comics on your nightstand, by the way."

Josie was sunshine, pure and simple. Being in her presence made you warm and content, but she would always be impossible to grasp. Basking in her glow was a heck of a consolation prize, though. Miles soaked in as much of her as he could.

"Yes," Josie declared.

"Yes, what?"

Josie grinned. "The date you were going to ask me on? My answer is yes."

EPILOGUE

GENERAL BRECKENRIDGE SURVEYED THE CONTENTS
of the military hangar and glowered. There were rows
after rows of specimens, each one worthy of its own
page-one write-up in the newspaper or magazine of
record in any country on the planet. Bodies of reptilian aliens lay on surgical tables. Strange bladed
weapons were stacked in heaps. Broken pieces of flying machines were being reassembled into complete
vehicles by teams of jump-suited technicians.

"How much have you recovered, General?" Dr.
Marisol Petri asked. Dr. Petri was a theoretical zoolo-
gist who'd been flown in from San Diego overnight.
She was only now getting her first look at the contents of the hangar where she'd be spending her
days and nights until General Breckenridge decided
otherwise. Which wasn't going to be anytime soon.

"There are two full cargo trucks still outside. I'm in the process of requisitioning a second hangar."

The enormous structure they were currently standing in at Dobbins Air Reserve Base was intended to house C-130 aircraft. The fact that there was more than enough alien material to fill it—and then some—was unsettling to say the least.

Another doctor was bent low over a reconstructed vehicle that looked like it could be Satan's WaveRunner. He waved a handheld device over the vehicle, and the readout squelched.

"Remarkable!" the doctor blurted. "Eight additions to the periodic table in less than ten minutes."

"Nine," a third doctor chirped from across the hangar.

"Nine! Shall I name an element after you, General? Perhaps Breckenridgetonium?"

General Breckenridge's mustache twitched. Had it been a horse's tail, he would've used it to swat the doctor like a pesky fly. "I'm not interested in scientific posterity, Doctor. I want to know where they're from and how they knew to come here."

The doctor cleared his throat. "Certainly. I'll get started immediately."

Breckenridge turned to Dr. Petri. "As for you, I want a full biological workup. What are their strengths? What are their weaknesses? Most important, what kills them?"

"I'll dissect as many specimens as you like, General, but it's going to take time."

"Time is the one thing I can't supply you with. I was told you specialize in the theoretical, so theorize." Breckenridge paused, reconsidering. "Just be sure your theories are correct."

Dr. Petri swallowed uneasily. "I'll do my best. Any particular specimen you'd like me to dissect first?"

"You misunderstand me, Doctor. I'm no longer interested in these . . . things." Breckenridge made a subtle hand gesture, indicating that the entire hangar and all its contents were beneath him. "I want to know about the other ones."

"General?" Dr. Petri scanned the hangar, as though she were wondering if a second species of alien was hidden in a footlocker somewhere.

Breckenridge pivoted on the toes of his impeccably polished shoes and leaned closer to Dr. Petri. "In case you haven't noticed, these aliens are dead. As such, they've ceased being my biggest concern. I want to know about the ones who defeated them. There were only a few dozen of them, if that, yet they crushed an entire invading force without suffering a single casualty. An invading force, I might add, that far exceeds the capability of our entire arsenal—army, navy, air force, and marine. Times ten."

Breckenridge paused to let his statement sink in.

He could tell by the way Dr. Petri had stopped blinking that she was scared. Good. She needed to be scared.

"Doctor, the carcasses and equipment we've gathered here have been in close proximity to the adversary. There'll be DNA. Tissue cells. Maybe a hair, if they have such a thing. Don't you concur?"

"It won't be easy, General. You're talking about finding a needle in a field of hay."

"That's precisely what I'm asking you to do. I've been saying it for decades, and as of yesterday, I finally have a president willing to agree with me. The entities with the golden capes represent the clearest and most present danger to the sovereignty of the United States of America."

Breckenridge glared through hawkish eyes. "Find me that needle, Doctor, and I'll stab it through their hearts. Starting with the one closest to home."

TURN THE PAGE FOR A SNEAK PEEK OF
THE THRILLING SEQUEL TO
ATTACK OF THE ALIEN HORDE.

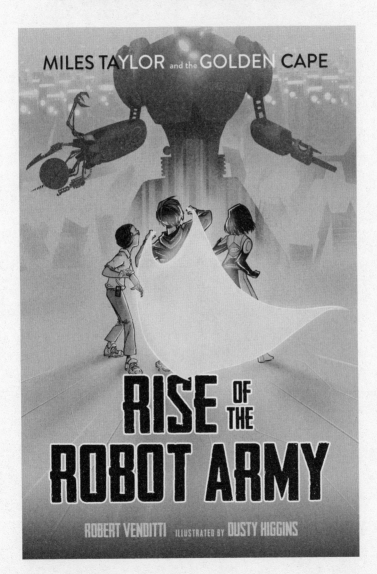

STOMACH GROWLING, MILES BOUNDED DOWN THE HALL
toward the kitchen. "Dad? Do I smell country ham?"

When Miles saw who was doing the cooking, he stopped short. It wasn't his dad at the stove. It was the next-door neighbor, Dawn Collins.

"Good nose," Dawn said, beaming. "Big day today, Mr. Eighth Grader. I told your dad I thought you could stand to start your morning right." She tipped a mixing bowl full of beaten eggs into a frying pan coated with a rich sheen of melted butter.

Mr. Taylor looked up from setting the table—Dixie plates and folded paper towels arranged with care. He rubbed a hand through his trimmed beard and shifted his feet. He seemed to get fidgety whenever Miles saw him and Dawn together, an increasingly common occurrence of late.

"I finally took Dawn up on her offer to fix us a meal. Isn't that neighborly of her?" Mr. Taylor locked eyes with Miles and nodded at Dawn, as if to prod Miles into giving a proper show of thanks.

Miles didn't need the prodding. "Absolutely."

Even before Mr. Taylor had become friendly with Dawn, Miles had liked her. She had a generous smile and made the best sweet tea he'd ever tasted. She was also the only person who'd welcomed Miles and Mr. Taylor when they'd moved into Cedar Lake Apartments the summer before Miles started seventh grade.

Up until a year ago, Dawn had been married to a no-account named Tom Collins. The last time Miles had seen him was the morning he'd overheard Mr. Collins berating Dawn for botching his breakfast. Worried for Dawn's safety, Miles had put on the cape for the first time and burst into apartment 2G as Gilded. He'd explained to Mr. Collins in no uncertain terms that he wasn't to be mean to Dawn ever again. Mr. Collins had lit out that afternoon, Dawn happily went from Mrs. to Ms., and Cedar Lake Apartments was all the better for it.

Watching Dawn drain bacon, stir eggs, and pull biscuits from the oven with ease, Miles couldn't help wondering if her treatment of Mr. Collins's breakfast had been a show of defiance. She definitely knew how to drive a stove.

"You two sit," Dawn said, turning off the burners. She carried the frying pan to the table and spooned eggs onto the plates.

You didn't have to tell a Taylor twice. Miles plopped his backpack on the floor and was reaching for his fork even before his butt hit the chair.

"Everything looks great, Dawn." Mr. Taylor smiled hungrily, pushing bacon and two biscuits onto his plate. He raised his plastic cup of orange juice. "A toast. To a breakfast that isn't toast."

Miles clunked his cup against his dad's. "I'll drink to that."

"Wait!" Dawn shrieked.

Mr. Taylor jolted and dropped a forkful of eggs onto his lap.

"I forgot the finishing touch." Dawn hurried to the freezer. She reached in and pulled out an ice cube tray. She cracked a pair of cubes shaped like peaches into each of their drinks. Dawn's prized collection of novelty ice cube molds was ever growing, and she seemed to have one for every occasion. If she was keeping her trays in Mr. Taylor's freezer, things were getting serious.

"Peaches?" Mr. Taylor asked, plucking the eggs from his work pants.

"August is National Peach Month," Dawn said

with a grin. "We do live in the Peach State, after all."

Every occasion.

Mr. Taylor shrugged. "Good enough for me. Sit down and join us. Miles and me can't polish off this spread by ourselves."

Dawn looked around hesitantly. "Um . . . where should I sit?"

Mr. Taylor had purchased their tiny dinette set for fifteen dollars at a garage sale because the full dining table from the old Taylor homestead was too big for the apartment. The set had come with only two chairs. This was the first time they'd ever needed a third.

"Shoot," Mr. Taylor said, frowning. "Here, take my spot." He started to stand.

Dawn placed a hand on his shoulder, easing him back down. "Nonsense. I need to leave for work anyway."

Dawn had recently earned a coveted waitressing spot during a shift with better tips at the Biscuit Barrel just down the street. Sinking his teeth into a piping-hot, scratch-made biscuit, Miles wondered how long it'd be before the manager wised up and had her switch aprons with the cook.

"You're on your own for cleanup," Dawn said. Then she leaned down and pecked Mr. Taylor on top of his head. With that, she was out the door.

Miles and his dad sat in uncomfortable silence. Mr. Taylor wouldn't look up, but Miles could tell his cheeks were burning red enough to fry eggs over easy. Mr. Taylor was embarrassed, like a kid caught smooching his girlfriend beneath the gym bleachers. Hollis and Dawn, sitting in a tree, K-I-S-S-I-N-G.

It was kind of awkward, Miles seeing his dad dating. Like he was peeking through a window at something he wasn't meant to watch. But it was kind of awesome, too. "It's okay, Dad," Miles said. "She's really nice. She's amazing, actually."

Mr. Taylor sat back in his chair, relieved. "She is, isn't she? Heck if I know what she wants with me." He smiled a bemused smile that Miles understood meant he was kidding but wasn't kidding, too. "Wooing girls has never been my strong suit. Just ask your mother." He leaned over his plate and forked a hunk of country ham.

"Think she can make corn bread?"

Corn bread was a Taylor favorite. Miles's mom had tried to make it once, but she'd baked it dry as a clay brick.

It wasn't that Miles's mom was bad. She was his mom, and he loved her. She and Miles's dad just weren't good together. No one was to blame—things just worked out that way sometimes.

Last Friday, when Miles had had his weekly phone call with his mom, he'd told her about Dawn. It had felt weird to talk about it with her, like he was telling her that her replacement had been hired.

Everyone deserves to be happy, she'd said.

Part of Miles wished her idea of happiness wasn't married to a CPA seven hundred miles away.

"I think Dawn can do just about anything," Mr. Taylor answered.

Mr. Taylor was entitled to happiness, too, and Miles truly hoped he'd found it. Sitting at their tiny table with a heaping breakfast between them, Miles thought about how far they'd come together. For the first time in a long time, everything seemed right with the world. Miles had a genuinely positive feeling. About himself. About life. About everything. The Taylor boys could take their lumps, but you couldn't keep them down.

"I've been meaning to talk to you," Mr. Taylor said. "About school."

Positive feeling: gone.

"Summer break is over. I gave you a lot of leeway these past three months, but it's time to get back to focusing on your studies. The days of being a super-hero all the time are over." Mr. Taylor glanced at the clock on the kitchen wall. "Eight twenty-two a.m., and I've already said something completely ludicrous. That might be a new record."

Right. In addition to Henry, Miles had also revealed to his dad that he was moonlighting as a superhero courtesy of the golden cape that—literally—could do no wrong. Miles remembered the stupefied expression on his dad's face the first time he saw Miles transform. It was the total opposite of the way his dad looked now, talking matter-of-factly about Miles's one-of-a-kind pastime over breakfast. Miles probably wasn't supposed to let his dad know, but he didn't beat himself up about it. Who was to say the old man who'd passed the Gilded mantle on to him hadn't ever told anyone? Sure, he'd instructed Miles not to, but grown-ups were notoriously espousing the do-as-I-say-not-as-I-do philosophy.

Besides, Miles hadn't had much choice. It was either let his dad know on the spot, or be forced to head for the hills with him and Dawn when the Unnd had attacked the city last fall. And anyway, there were more than seven billion people in the world, but Miles had told only a measly two. All things considered, he had a pretty good average. He hadn't even told Josie Campobasso. If that wasn't a heroic show of restraint, what was?

Josie. If there was one person Miles wanted to let in on his secret, it was Josie. She was the most perfect girl to ever set foot—

"Miles? Are you listening?" Mr. Taylor asked.

"Hm?"

"I said, when seventh grade ended, you and I made a deal. I'd lay off and let you have the summer to practice with the cape. Get more comfortable with the heavy workload of looking after the city, so you could be ready when something really bad happens. Tell you the truth, I couldn't be prouder of how you've done. But you're in eighth grade now. Your last year before high school. I want you focusing on your schoolwork first and foremost. Let the police and fire department handle what they can. Your job is to handle what they can't. And *only* what they can't.

"You do that, and when the big things come up, I'll cover for you missing school. Which, unless I'm mistaken, makes me the only dad in America who'll help his thirteen-year-old cut class. Remember that come Father's Day."

"I know it's not easy, Dad. Dealing with me being Gilded. So thanks."

Miles meant it. When it came to fatherhood, this was seriously uncharted territory. It wasn't like Mr.

Taylor could go to the library and check out *The Single Parent's Guide to Raising a Superhero.*

Mr. Taylor set down his fork. "I understand you have important boots to fill—Lord, isn't that an understatement—but I want your word it won't get in the way of school any more than it has to." Mr. Taylor held forward his hand. "Let's shake on it."

In the Taylor household, shaking hands sealed an agreement tighter than a presidential signature.

Miles clasped Mr. Taylor's hand. "I promise, Dad." He felt a pang of loss. A few months ago the summer had seemed to stretch out in front of him like an endless highway. Now all that road was in his rearview. How had it gone by so fast?

Mr. Taylor went back to his breakfast. "Good man. After eighth grade comes high school. After that, college. Not a bit of that is negotiable. Because, unless there's something you're not telling me, being Gilded isn't ever going to put food on your table."

Another truth. For all the cape's abilities, making money wasn't one of them. Using it for personal profit was another no-no. All the comic books, toys, and other merchandise based on Gilded were done without consent. Henry had explained the legalese of it to Miles. Something to do with Gilded being a public figure like the president, so his likeness wasn't protected. It sounded fishy, but what was Miles going to do about it, file a lawsuit?

"But what if—"

"I don't want to hear it. My tax bill hasn't gone down, so I'm guessing that means there's still cops and firefighters in this town. Let them do what they get paid to. You think dispatch sends me out every time someone needs to replace a lightbulb?"

"No."

"Darn right, no. I handle the big jobs. Everyone else can pitch in on the rest. That's what I expect of you."

"All right," Miles said glumly. "I will."

"I expect so. Don't forget you gave me your word on this. A man doesn't have his word—"

"—he doesn't have jack." A tried-and-true Hollis Taylor proverb. Right up there with "Better to have it and not need it than to need it and not have it" and "If you don't like Johnny Cash music, I don't want to know you."

Miles pushed his half-eaten breakfast around on his plate. All this talk of not being Gilded had ruined his appetite. He stood from the table. "Speaking of school, I'd better get going. The bus will be here soon."

"You sure?" Mr. Taylor looked surprised. "No telling when we'll eat like this again."

"Yeah. I'm not hungry."

"You go on, then. Have a good day. As for me"—
Mr. Taylor reached for Miles's plate—"I vow to not let this good bacon go to waste."

Miles picked up his backpack. The backpack that went everywhere he did. The backpack that held far more than books and notebook paper. He settled it onto his shoulders, feeling the soft hum of its contents against his body.

All his worries vanished. No matter what else happened, he was Gilded. And as long as that was true, nothing could ever go wrong.

Did you LOVE reading this book?

Visit the Whyville...

Where you can:

- Discover great books!
- Meet new friends!
- Read exclusive sneak peeks and more!

Log on to visit now!
bookhive.whyville.net

a Numedeon, Inc. property

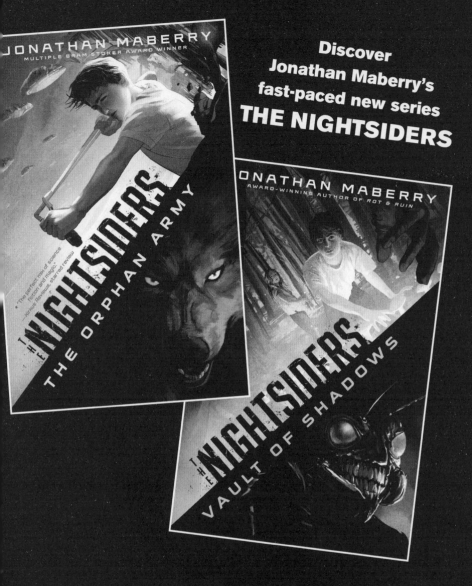

Discover
Jonathan Maberry's
fast-paced new series
THE NIGHTSIDERS

★"The perfect mix of science fiction and magic."
–*Kirkus Reviews*, starred review

Fast, frightful, and fantastic—a faerie story like no other."
–Dan Abnett, writer of the *Guardians of the Galaxy* comic for Marvel

PRINT AND EBOOK EDITIONS AVAILABLE
From Simon & Schuster Books for Young Readers
simonandschuster.com/kids

THE HIGHER INSTITUTE OF VILLAINOUS EDUCATION

H.I.V.E.

DON'T GET MAD, GET EVIL.

FROM MARK WALDEN

PRINT AND EBOOK EDITIONS AVAILABLE

From Simon & Schuster Books for Young Readers
KIDS.SimonandSchuster.com